RETURN TO SENDER

J. S. COOPER

BLURB

Return to Sender

When Savannah Carter takes a job as a personal assistant in upstate New York, she never expects to be working for a man like Wade Hart. With his sparkling green eyes and devious smile, he is a man she both hates and adores. When their professional relationship becomes more intimate, Savannah is ecstatic … until she hears a phone call that changes everything.

"I never should have hired her, she can ruin everything."

Those words whispered by Wade on the phone shock her, but before she can confront him about what she's heard, he disappears, leaving only a cryptic note behind.

Suddenly Savannah's "too good to be true" job seems to be exactly that. What are the secrets that Wade is hiding from her? How is she a threat to him? And just who is her mysterious new friend Gordon, and why is he so insistent on being in her life?

While Savannah's heart is falling for Wade, her brain is

telling her to run. Can the man who ignites her hidden passions be her happily ever after? Or should she heed the warnings and run back to New York City before she gets burned?

CHAPTER 1

"I've fucked up, Henry. I can never let her know the truth. This whole thing was a mistake. A huge mistake. I never should have created that ad. She can destroy everything. Absolutely everything. I never should have let Savannah Carter into our lives. If she learns the truth, our lives will be ruined."

I trembled as I stood there. I knew I should say something—anything. I needed to let Wade know that I was there and listening, but I was too scared. The lack of emotion in his voice made me shiver. What was he talking about? What did he mean by saying his life would be ruined if I learned the truth? What truth? And then I remembered his mother's note. What had she said exactly? Something about me not knowing everything and not being good enough for her son. And had she mentioned bodies being buried in the forest or was I remembering that incorrectly? I chewed on my lower lip, wishing now that I hadn't ripped up the note.

I stepped back into the bathroom and walked back into the shower, allowing the water to warm my shivering body. My fingers went to my breasts and rubbed Wade's dry cum off of my skin. Just moments ago, being with him had felt so sexy, and I had felt so wanted. Being in his arms had felt magical. Now, as my fingers moved to my thighs and between my legs, I wondered who this man was that I had let touch me so intimately. Already I could feel a hollow ache between my legs wanting to be filled again, but it now the feeling was tainted by unease. What secrets was Wade hiding from me? And how could I ruin everything?

Memories and thoughts rushed through my mind as the water ran down my body. I knew the smart thing to do would be to leave, but I knew that I couldn't. I was already too far in. I had given myself to him, and I wanted more. Wade was like a drug: dangerous but addictive. I wanted him in my veins.

The very thought of him made me shiver with nervous anticipation.

Wade poked his head through the bathroom door. "Hey, Savannah, are you coming out anytime today? I'm hungry."

"Feel free to start eating without me," I shouted over the sound of the water. I stood very still, wondering if he was going to join me in the shower. I hoped he couldn't tell from my voice that something had changed in the minutes we'd been apart.

"I can't." His voice got closer and I trembled again despite the steam.

"Why not? I brought the pizza into the room. You can go ahead and eat without me."

"That's not what I want to eat." He opened the shower door and stared at me, his eyes glittering with an odd intensity. I trembled under his gaze and wanted to roll my eyes at myself. Was I a fair maiden from the 1500s?

"Now, are you nearly done or what?" His eyes ravished my body and the steamy air between us crackled with lust.

Despite everything, I couldn't help smiling at him. "I'll

be out soon. Is everything okay?" My small attempt to figure out what was going on felt weak, even to myself.

"Why wouldn't it be?" There's a smile on his face still, but there was something flinty in his eyes. All I had to do was tell him I'd heard his conversation with Henry, but something held me back. Maybe it was because I didn't think he would tell me the truth. Maybe it was because I was worried about what he'd say if he knew I'd been eavesdropping. Maybe it was because I was scared to hear something that would turn me off forever. Or maybe, and this was an even scarier thought, what he had to tell me would be awful and I still wouldn't be able to bring myself to leave.

"I don't know." I shrugged. "Did I scare you off by saying I loved you?"

"You don't love me." He shook his head, the smile dropping for a few seconds. "That was post-coital bliss talking, that's all."

"That's it, huh?" I didn't know whether to be offended that he was dismissing my feelings, though I almost hoped he was correct. I didn't want to be in love with this man. No matter how good of a love maker he was.

"Yeah, that's it." He blinked a couple of times and then he said softly. "I have to go away for a bit. I'll leave you instructions on what to do while I'm gone."

"What do you mean, go away for a bit?"

"I mean I have to take a trip. I need to take care of some business." His eyes shifted away from me. "I'll be gone a week or two, maybe more."

"I see." Though I really didn't. Why hadn't he mentioned this trip before? He was my boss— surely it would have slipped that he had a business trip today? What was going on here?

"Are you going to miss me?" he teased as he took a step into the shower.

3

"Hmmm, I'm not sure." I splashed him with some water. "I'm trying to shower, Wade."

"Don't you mean, The Wade?"

"No, there is no way I'm calling you The Wade." I rolled my eyes. "Or The Wade Hart, either." I gasped as he pulled me toward him and kissed my neck. "Don't you think you should take your boxers off?"

"I thought you could do that for me." He chuckled as his hand slid around my waist. "And then there are a few more things you could do for me as well." His hand moved down to my ass and squeezed. "Though maybe we should get you some real food first. We need to ensure you've got enough energy."

"I think I'd like that." My stomach growled in agreement.

"Are you hungry or just really excited to see me?" He chuckled and brushed back the wet hair that was plastered across my face so that he could stare into my eyes. "Sometimes I look at you and I can't quite believe how beautiful you are."

"I'm not beautiful." I reached up and touched his face. "You're the beautiful one."

He grinned. "I prefer the term handsome."

"Why? Don't you like to be called beautiful?"

"Ruggedly sexy, yes. Handsome as sin, yes. Sex on legs, yes. Beautiful, no." He wrinkled his nose. "Beauty is delicate and sweet, like you. I'm anything but."

"So, you're saying you're not delicate and sweet?"

"Would you say that I'm delicate and sweet?"

"No." I chewed on my lower lip and pressed myself against him. "Is there anything you want to tell me, Wade?" I asked softly, praying he would laugh and say something like, *Savannah, I never intended on falling in love and you've ruined my lifelong dream of being a bachelor.* That would make everything okay. That would mean that he wasn't messed up in anything bad.

"Tell you?" He looked confused. "You mean like what I want to eat tomorrow?"

"No." I grabbed the soap and looked away from him. Did he really think I cared about what he wanted to eat tomorrow? As if feeding him were the first thing on my mind after giving myself to him for the first time in my life. *Thanks for taking my virginity, Wade. Oh, and would you like fries with that?*

I bit down on my lower lip to stifle a giggle that threatened to burst out of me. It wasn't funny, really, but I felt like I was on the verge of hysteria. My body was still buzzing from what Wade and I had just done, and I wanted a moment to enjoy it before I started to analyze the conversation I'd just heard. So much had happened, so many thoughts and feelings were rushing through me, and I felt like I needed a chance to catch up.

"Savannah, are you okay?" Wade's voice was soft, but there was a strange harshness to his expression. "Are you upset? Do you regret what we did?" He sounded sad. "Do you think I took advantage of—"

"Not at all." I stepped forward and touched his chest. "I wanted you. I wanted you to be my first. I wanted it all."

"Good." He leaned down and kissed me. "You're a special girl, Savannah."

I wanted to ask him if that was really true, but I didn't dare. I wasn't sure if I wanted to know the answer. Sometimes it was better to not ask questions if you weren't sure if you'd like the answers.

CHAPTER 2

The warm sunlight on my face woke me up, and I stretched happily in the luxurious sheets before turning on my side. I frowned when I noticed that Wade's side of the bed was empty.

I listened for the sound of water running in the bathroom, but I heard nothing, so he wasn't in the shower. I sat up in the bed and carefully pulled down the sheets to study my naked body. I looked the same, even if I didn't feel the same. There was a slight ache between my legs, a fullness and a roughness that I'd never felt before, but it wasn't unpleasant. If anything, it just reminded me of the fact that Wade had been inside of me the night before. My face flushed red as I thought about the fact that I'd lost my virginity to Wade Hart. In the light of the day, it almost felt surreal to think that we'd made love. It had been magical. Even though it had initially hurt, the pleasure I'd experienced was definitely something I could get used to.

"Wade!" I pulled the sheet off of the bed and wrapped it around my naked body as I got out of bed. "Wade, are you in there?" I peered into the bathroom, but it was dark and empty. Maybe he'd gone to the kitchen to make me breakfast in bed. I grinned at the thought. I hoped he was making pancakes. Blueberry pancakes. That would be delicious. I opened the door and poked my head into the hallway.

"Wade, are you in the kitchen?" I waited for a response, but none came. Frowning, I walked down the hallway towards the kitchen. It was empty. "Damn it." I made my way to the French doors and went outside to see if he was swimming. I pictured Wade and I making love in the pool but soon realized he wasn't there either.

"Where the hell are you?" I mumbled to myself as I walked back into the house. I made my way to the fridge to grab some orange juice and it was then that I saw an envelope with my name on it on the table, propped up next to a glass. A sense of foreboding filled me as I and picked it up. I ripped it open and pulled out a letter.

To Ms. Savannah Carter,

I have to go away for a week or so. My mother will also be gone. There is a stack of files on the desk in the library for you to deal with. I will email you soon with some more tasks.

Sincerely,

The Wade Hart (or, as you called me last night, Big Daddy)

"I never called you big daddy, asshole." I dropped the letter onto the table. Why hadn't he told me that he had to go out of town first thing in the morning? Wasn't that something you would have told your assistant? I chewed on my lower lip. Maybe he'd left because of me. Maybe he regretted having sex with me. Or rather, regretted the fact that he'd had sex with me and I'd been a virgin.

"And you told him you thought you loved him," I groaned. "Why, Savannah, why?" Tears pricked the back of my eyelids. Had I been used for a night of hot sex? Was Wade now scared that I might have developed real feelings? "Ms. Savannah Carter" didn't exactly sound intimate.

I took a deep breath and headed to my room. I would not let myself cry. I would not allow myself to wallow and feel sorry about what had happened. I had made a decision and I had enjoyed that decision. Wade hadn't promised me anything and I hadn't promised him anything. In fact, he had been nothing but honest about what we were doing. Well, that wasn't exactly true. He hadn't been completely honest. Not if his words of the previous night had been correct. What had I heard him saying again? *I've fucked up, Henry. I can never let her know the truth. This whole thing was a mistake. A huge mistake. I never should have created that ad. She can destroy everything. Absolutely everything. I never should have let Savannah Carter into our lives. If she learns the truth, our lives will be ruined.*

I wished now that I'd marched into the room and demanded to know what he'd been talking about. It wasn't as if I'd been deliberately eavesdropping on him. And it wasn't as if he could lie about the conversation if he'd known I'd heard him. But whatever it was, Henry knew as well. And Henry was a sweetheart. He wouldn't be involved in anything nefarious, would he? But as I opened my bedroom door, I realized I really had no idea if Henry could be involved in anything bad. I barely knew the man.

I decided to have a shower and call Lucy. She'd be shocked, of course. I mean, I'd been shocked as well. I felt slightly guilty and slightly giddy as I thought about my call with Lucy. What would she say, and would she hate Wade when I told her about the conversation I'd overheard?

"Stop overthinking it, Savannah," I lectured myself as I walked into the bathroom. "It is what it is, and what it will be is up to you."

⚜

"Lucy, are you sitting down?" I knew I sounded melodramatic, but if there was ever a time in my life that I could justify being dramatic, it was now.

"No, I'm walking Jolene and I'm not about to sit down in the street. Why?"

"I'm about to tell you something absolutely crazy." I could have been Lady Macbeth the way my voice was carrying across the room. "Sorry, let me speak a little bit quieter. How's Jolene doing, by the way? Shall we Facetime?"

"Like I said, I'm in the street." Lucy laughed. "I know there are many things that pass in New York City, but I don't want to be one of those rude people carrying on a video conversation while I'm walking down the street with my dog that is stopping to piss every few seconds." She paused. "Also, I thought it was only male dogs that marked their territory? Jolene is trying to piss on every pole we see."

"She's an alpha." I laughed. "And she's probably horny. She wants all the male dogs to smell her."

Lucy groaned.

"Erm, talking about horny …" I knew my segue wasn't the smoothest, but I was dying to tell her about my night.

"I didn't know that we were talking about horny—" Lucy gasped. "Jolene, no! Jolene, come here! Ugh, this dog!"

"Sorry, Lucy, but thank you for taking care of her." I felt guilty as I knew that Jolene wasn't the easiest dog to walk. "I totally owe you. When I get back to the city, I'll buy you a Cartier watch or a Gucci bag or something."

"Actually, I'd love a Ferragamo studio bag in pine green. This actress came into the office and she had one, and it was to die for. It's made from ostrich leather. Did you even know there was such a thing?"

"Ostrich leather? What?" I laughed. "Do they have to skin the ostriches? I can't imagine it looks good. They're such ugly creatures."

"No idea, but it is to die for, I tell you. Absolutely gorgeous, and it's only ten grand." She burst out laughing. "Can you believe I said it's only ten grand, what world am I living in?"

"I slept with Wade!" I burst out, not able to hold it in anymore.

"You what?" It was Lucy's turn to shout. "Did I hear you correctly? You had THE SEX with Wade Hart?"

"Well, technically I had the sex with The Wade Hart." I giggled.

"Oh, my days, I do need to sit down." Lucy sounded shocked. "Tell me all. Did it hurt? Was it amazing? Do you feel different? Do you love him?"

"Yes, it hurt a little but not for long. Yes, it was so amazing. I feel kinda different, and ugh, I don't want to talk about love." I paused and lowered my voice. "So now I have the exciting bit out of the way, I need to be more serious. There's something weird going on here."

"Oh God, please don't tell me this is a sex trafficking situation. I was starting to wonder when—"

I cut her off. "No, Lucy. At least I don't think it has anything to do with that. Though I wouldn't be surprised if there was something a bit sinister going on."

"What do you mean?" Lucy's breath was coming faster now and I could tell she was walking quickly. I had a feeling that she was hurrying to get home so that she could scream at me.

"So last night after we'd, uhm, done the deed …"

"Don't be a prude now, Savannah." Lucy laughed. "It's fine to say 'after you had sex.'"

"Yeah, well, *after*, I went to have a shower and I needed a towel, and so I was going back to the room, but I opened the door and he was on the phone."

"Oh God, please do not tell me he was married," Lucy growled. "These men suck, why can't they just be faithful?'

"It wasn't his wife. I don't think he has a wife." But even as I said the words it struck me that perhaps I was wrong. Maybe he was married, and that was why he'd said I would ruin his life. But no, he hadn't said *his* life, singular. He'd said "*our* lives will be ruined," as in his and Henry's. What would Henry care if his married brother had an affair? That wouldn't affect his life in any way.

"Savannah, are you sure?"

"I'm pretty sure he's not married. Hold on, let me think about his exact words, and you can tell me what you think."

"Okay, hold on a few minutes. I just got back home. Going to take the elevator up to the apartment, give Jolene some water, and then I'll be ready."

"Okay." I nodded absentmindedly as I walked out of my room and down the hallway. The house was quiet, almost ominously so, without Wade in it. I held the phone to my ear and thought for a few seconds before heading to the library. It was the only space that really felt like mine on this estate. Even more than my bedroom. Maybe because I spent so much time there.

Sounding a little breathless, Lucy came back on the line. "Okay, I'm back. Now tell me everything."

"Well, I've essentially told you everything, but these were his words as best as I can remember them, 'I never should have hired her, she can ruin everything.' That's what he said."

"Is that *all* he said?"

"No, he said, 'I've fucked up, Henry. I can never let her know the truth. This whole thing was a mistake. A huge mistake. I never should have created that ad. She can destroy everything. Absolutely everything. I never should have let Savannah Carter into our lives. If she learns the truth, our lives will be ruined.'" I paused and bit down on my lower lip. "Can't remember if I told you before, but Henry is his little brother."

"Yeah, you mentioned him." Lucy's voice was low. "What can you destroy?"

"I don't know!"

"And you're alone? He left you?"

"Yes."

"I'm coming up."

"What?"

"I'm catching the train, and I'm coming up with Jolene."

"Are you sure?"

"Savannah, my best friend took a job on a country estate with some hot weirdo. He has proceeded to take her virginity, disappear, and now he's telling his brother that she could ruin everything. There is no way in hell I'm leaving you there alone, and I know I can't convince you to come home right now."

"You don't know that." Though of course she did. If I'd had any intention of going home, I would have called her from the train. Instead, I was sitting at a chair in the library, wondering what I'd find if I continued searching through the rest of the books.

"Savannah Carter, I have lived with you long enough to know how your mind works. Will you be able to collect me from the train station or do I need to hire a car?"

"I can pick you up. Are you sure you can come? What about work?"

"You're more important. Plus I'm sure Jolene would love to see you."

"I miss my little baby. I hope she hasn't been too bad."

"If by bad, you mean she peed on my towel and ate half of my burger last night, then no, of course not." Lucy's voice was dry. "You know that dog, Savannah. I'm not going to list the reasons why Jolene is on my shit list right now."

"Oh no, I'm so sorry, Lucy. But I'm excited to see you and Jolene. I've missed you."

"I've missed you as well. I'm excited for us to get to the bottom of this mystery, and I want to meet all these hot guys you keep talking about."

"I wouldn't say hot guys plural." I laughed. "I mean Wade is hot and Henry is also hot, and Gordon is really good looking too, but I mean—"

"You mean what?" She laughed. "You can't have all three of them. What about me?"

"Do you really want a Hart brother? After what I've just told you?"

"Most probably not, but it could make my life really exciting." She giggled. "I want some excitement and hot sex as well."

"True, the sex was hot."

"Oh, I just can't believe it. Savannah Carter, you're a woman."

"What was I before? A dog?" I paused. "Don't answer that." I laughed. "I know what Wade's answer would be to that."

"I hope I get to meet him." Lucy sounded thoughtful. "Also, when I come, we're going to play detective. I think we need to figure out just what Wade was talking about before you become anymore invested in him."

I sighed. "I'm already invested, Lucy. I'm scared I'm going to get my heart broken."

"That's why it's much better for me to be there than not." She paused then and I knew that she was thinking very carefully about what to say next. I leaned back in the chair, waiting. As I did, I noticed a piece of paper on the ground and got up to pick it up. I opened it and read quickly, my cheeks flushing as I did so.

"Oh my God, listen to this Lucy."

"What?"

"I just found another note from Wade."

"Another note?"

"Yup, it was on the floor in the library. It says, 'If you're thinking about snooping, don't even bother. Just look after the house while I'm gone and write your poetry. If you're bored, why don't you learn a dance to surprise me with when I get back home.'" I gasped. "What a cheek!"

"He really is a condescending asshole, isn't he?" Lucy said. "And he sounds scared. What doesn't he want you to find out?"

"I don't know." And then, because it had been on my mind a lot in the last couple of days, I said, "I wonder if it has to do with his last assistant."

"What about her?"

"He just doesn't really seem to say much about her. I wonder if something happened."

"Like what?"

"Oh, I don't know ..." My voice trailed off, for while I didn't know, I had plenty of thoughts. "What if he killed her?"

"Savannah, no! What are you talking about?" Lucy's voice was shrill. "You're not seriously entertaining that thought, are you?"

"No ... I mean, I don't think so." I chewed on my lower

lip. "But you can never tell who might be a killer. Aren't we always surprised when we watch those Aurora Teagarden movies on Hallmark?"

"Savannah, that's a TV show. Those are actors. It's not real."

"Well, I know that. I'm just saying. Sometimes the bad guys surprise you."

"You're making me even more nervous for you now. Let me pack some stuff and see about the train. In the meantime, can you call that friend of yours and see if he can hang out? I'm not sure I want you to be there by yourself right now."

"Okay." I nodded. "I can call Gordon. Actually, I'm pretty sure he'd love to see the Hart house. He seems to be slightly obsessed with it."

"What do you mean by obsessed?" Lucy sounded tense. "Is everyone you know straight out of a Lifetime movie?"

"Oh, I guess the Hart family is just well known in Herne Hill Village and everyone seems to want to be in the know. Gordon just told me he'd always wanted to see the estate. I guess all of us commoners want to see how the other half live."

"Yeah, I guess." Lucy didn't sound convinced. "Well, I'm going to go now, but you call me if anything comes up okay? I'll let you know what time I'm going to be arriving at the train station."

"Sounds good, Lucy. I can't wait to see you and Jolene."

"We can't wait to see you as well." And with that, she was gone.

I walked over to the window to look outside. The day had turned gloomy and foreboding and the dark sky made me shudder. I stared at the vast forest in front of me and wondered what animals lived in its midst. It suddenly struck me that I was alone in a private house in the middle of nowhere. I touched the windowpane and I wondered what I looked like from outside the house. If someone was looking up and saw me, a lone figure, with a pale face and worried expression, they might think I was a ghost.

I knew I was being dramatic, but the moment seemed to call for some drama. I suddenly recalled a poem that I'd read in college, and I recited it as I gazed out of the window.

"O Rose thou art sick.
    The invisible worm,
    That flies in the night
In the howling storm:

Has found out thy bed
    Of crimson joy:
    And his dark secret love
Does thy life destroy."

"And his dark secret love, does thy life destroy," I repeated as I stepped back from the window. I shivered as the last words left my lips. "Oh, William Blake, what were you thinking when you wrote 'The Sick Rose'?" I whispered to myself.

To think that just last night, Wade Hart had been inside of me. I had given him what he wanted, eagerly and so wantonly. Even the memory left me longing for more. I had given my body to a man whose life I could destroy… and I had absolutely no idea how.

CHAPTER 3

"Hey, Savannah, how are you?" Gordon answered the phone in his usual cheerful tone.

I smiled. At least he was someone that I could trust and not worry about. "Hey, I'm good. What are you doing? Did you want to come over for lunch?"

"Oh, I'd love to. Will I get to meet the elusive Wade as well?"

"No, he's out of town right now."

"He is?" He sounded surprised. "Where did he go?"

"He's my boss. He doesn't tell me all of his whereabouts." I knew I sounded snooty, but I was feeling a bit defensive. Where the hell was Wade? And why hadn't he told me?

"Yeah, he's a secretive guy. Maybe he's gone to visit one of his many women." Gordon laughed.

Jealousy surged through me. "What do you mean, one of his many women? I thought he was single!"

Was that where he'd gone then? To be with his other woman? If that were the case, I'd show him when he got back that he'd messed with the wrong woman. Though I wasn't sure what I'd do. I had a feeling if I cut up his clothes or started a fire, I'd be in jail faster than I could say, "You're a cheater, Wade Hart." And honestly, I couldn't even really call him a cheater. How could it be cheating if we weren't even really in a relationship?

"I'm joking," Gordon said quickly. "I'd love to come over, but why don't you let me take you for lunch? I don't want you to have to cook for me."

"Oh, it wouldn't be a big deal. I don't mind."

"No, but I would feel bad. Meet me at the cafe in town at noon and then we can go back to the house."

"Sounds good." I was happy at the idea of leaving the house. Maybe some fresh air would help to clear my head. "I'll get some work done and then meet up with you later, okay?"

"Okay. Bye, Savannah. I look forward to seeing you later."

There was something in his tone that made me pause as I put the phone down. I didn't think I was particularly psychic or attuned to vibes, but something felt wrong. I couldn't put my finger on it. I didn't know if it was related to Gordon or my overall situation with Wade, but something felt off.

"Who are you, Sabrina the Teenage Witch?" I shook my head at my thoughts. I decided to go back to Wade's room to see if I could find any clues as to what was going on. I wasn't going to snoop—well, that was a lie. I *was* going to snoop, but I was entitled to snoop. If there was ever a time a woman was entitled to snoop, this was it. I just had to find out what was going on.

The first thing I noticed in his room was the big bed with the messy sheets. I supposed I should wash them or something. Or at least make the bed.

"Yeah, right." I giggled. "That's not my concern right now." I walked over to the bed and then lifted up the pillows. I wasn't sure what I expected to find underneath them, but there was nothing there. Then I looked at the side tables, opening the drawers and rifling through the contents quickly. I felt slightly guilty, but it wasn't like I was trying to steal trade secrets or something. To be fair, Wade's drawers were quite boring. And then I got to the bottom drawer and my jaw fell open.

"Wow, what do we have here?" I pulled out a pair of handcuffs and a steel object that reminded me of a pinwheel. I ran my fingers across the sharp edges and pricked myself. "Ouch!"

I put it on the top of the night table and then reached back into the drawer and pulled out some silk scraps and some beads. "Whoa." I touched them lightly. I knew these were anal beads, not that I'd used them before. And then I saw a butt plug. My eyebrows shot up and I could feel my face reddening. How many women had he used that with? I chewed on my lower lip wondering what it would be like to do that with him. I couldn't even imagine it. It seemed even more intimate than normal intercourse. But somehow with Wade I could imagine it being pleasurable and hot. That naughty, forbidden sort of pleasure that made you feel that maybe being bad was the best kind of good there could be.

I put the stuff back in the drawer and moved over to the closets. As I walked, I passed a bookshelf that I'd never really noticed before. It was about five feet tall, made of reclaimed wood with leather straps, and was full of books. I stopped to look at what books Wade read, feeling a surge of surprise when I realized what they were. I'd never thought of Wade as being a big reader. He had never paid much attention to the books in the library, and I'd just assumed that meant he wasn't really interested, but as I picked up a stack of books from the top shelf, I began to wonder.

I looked through the books: *1984* by George Orwell, *The Lord of The Rings* by J. R. R. Tolkien, *Catch-22* by Joseph

Heller, *And Then There Were None* by Agatha Christie, and *Don Quixote* by Miguel de Cervantes. Were these were his favorites?

The Agatha Christie book seemed a little out of place; I wondered if he was into mysteries in general or just Agatha Christie. I held the books in my hand feeling like I was getting new insight into Wade's mind when I noticed a small note card on the shelf. I put the books back and grabbed the card.

It appeared to be a grocery list. There were only five items listed: white bread, butter, American cheese, cheddar cheese, and salt and vinegar potato chips. I frowned as I reread it. I'd never seen this list before and he'd never asked me to get any of these items. Why would he have a list for bread and cheese? I put the notecard back on the shelf and then went to look in his closet and through his pants pockets. I knew I was being invasive, but I wanted more information, and I wanted it now.

Just who was Wade Hart? And what did his secrets mean for me?

"I've got an evening ticket." Lucy sounded pleased with herself. "Jolene and I will arrive at nine p.m. I hope that's okay?"

"That's perfect," I said to the car as I drove. I always felt weird conversing with people using Bluetooth. It made me feel a bit like a crazy person, just talking into the air. "I'm off to meet Gordon for lunch, and then we're going to go back to Wade's place."

"Oh, to look for clues?"

"No, just to hang out. I'm not sure how much I want to tell him. I like him and he's always been so friendly to me, but there's just something about him that puts my back up, you know?"

"You don't think he's a psychopath, do you?"

"No, Lucy! How many psychopaths do you think there are in Herne Hill Village?"

"Well, we have three contenders already," she pointed out. "Wade, Henry, and Gordon."

"Henry's not a psychopath."

"Well, you never know. If he's related to Wade, anything is possible."

"He's really nice and really quite handsome." I pulled onto the main road. "In fact, I kinda wish he was staying at the house as well."

"You dirty dog!"

"Nothing like that." I giggled. "I can't see myself having a threesome."

"I wasn't even thinking of a threesome."

"What were you thinking of?"

"I was thinking you were saying you would have hooked up with him instead of Wade, not that you'd thought about doing both of them at the same time."

"I've never thought of that!" I laughed. "Just because I've lost my virginity doesn't mean I'm ready to be a freak."

"Get your freak on, I say." Lucy giggled.

"Isn't that a Missy Elliott song?"

"Maybe, and I'm sure she'd approve."

"You want me to sleep with two brothers?"

"Imagine the poetry you could write then!"

"Lucy, you're an idiot."

"Anything for the art, Savannah, and then I could make a movie and it would become an instant hit and we'd both be rich and famous forever."

"Yeah." I laughed. "I'm sure everyone wants to hear about

me banging two hot brothers with some super-secret shady past."

"Did you find anything out about that?"

"No, but I did find something odd …"

"What's that?"

"I found a shopping list but it contained items Wade has never asked me to get."

"Oh boy, let me guess, oil and jelly."

"Oil and jelly?"

"You know what I mean. Massage oil and KY jelly."

I groaned in response. "Lucy, sometimes you're the most immature person I know."

"Sorry, I couldn't resist." She laughed. "And I'm not really the *most* immature, am I?"

"No, you're not." I agreed. "You only wear that crown half of the year."

"And you wear it the other half."

"Not something that I'm proud of," I admitted ruefully. It wasn't that we were immature per se, it was just that we were young and impressionable and very, very goofy. "I'm excited to see you. Do you want to go to an open mic night?"

"Do you think we'll have time?"

"Hopefully. I mean, there's not much else going on up here."

"Asides from you doing Wade Hart."

"Yes, asides from that. And that can't happen right now anyway because he's disappeared."

"And because he's holding a deep, dark secret. Don't forget the deep, dark secret."

"How could I?" I began looking for a parking spot. "I have to go, Lucy, I just got into the village and I'm going to park and meet up with Gordon. I'll speak to you later?"

"Yes. Can't wait to see you."

"Can't wait to see you, too."

RETURN TO SENDER

I smiled into the air and the music started playing again as Lucy hung up. I was excited to see Lucy and Jolene again. I wanted them to see where I lived, what I'd been doing, and I wanted to hug them both. I could feel the buzz of excitement in my veins. It would be so comforting to have a piece of home here with me.

I found a parking spot and then headed to the diner. I walked in and looked around but I didn't see Gordon.

"Howdy." Beryl walked over to me, a pen in her hair and a curious look in her eyes. "Can I help you?"

"Yes, my friend and I would like to grab lunch. He should be here soon."

"Hmmm." She pursed her lips and then mumbled something under her breath.

"Sorry, I didn't hear you."

"You've been making all sorts of friends since you've been here, haven't you?"

"Well, I wouldn't say that, no." I shook my head and followed her to a table. "Do you have any specials today or can I get anything on the menu?" I looked up at her as she placed two menus on the table.

"We always serve everything on the menu." She took her pen out from behind her ear and tapped it on the table. "Mr. Wade going to be joining us?"

"No," I shook my head. "He's out of town."

"Is he now?" She raised an eyebrow. "Hmm."

"Do you know him well?"

"Mr. Wade?" She shook her head. "Not really. We knew his father, though. He used to come in here all the time."

"Oh really? With Wade and Henry?"

"Not so much." She shook her head. "T'is a sad thing what happened."

"What happened?"

23

"You know with his wife, and the business." She shrugged. "Nearly lost everything, they did."

"Oh?" I asked her curiously. "But I guess he worked it out?"

"He worked it out, all right." She nodded. "Yup."

"Wade and Henry seem like nice men." I decided to see if I could prod some information out of her. She had to know something. Hadn't she been warning me at the pub that the Hart men were no good?

"They seem to be fine."

"Were they close with their father?"

"Not really."

"Did they have a big funeral for him?"

"A funeral?" Her eyes widened and she stared at me for a few seconds without blinking. "Death is a funny thing, isn't it? It can bring so much heartache, and in other ways so much joy."

"Joy?" I blinked. Who would be happy that someone died?

"You're meeting that boy Gordon?" Her face grew tighter as I nodded. "You be careful, you hear."

"Careful of what?"

"There's a lot of secrets in this town." She leaned forward and looked me in the eyes. "There's things that people don't want to get out. And there's people that will use you to make sure that—" Suddenly she stopped talking and straightened up. Her gaze flew to the door that had just opened. Gordon was walking into the restaurant, a big smile on his face as he headed towards me. Beryl looked at him and then back at me. "You just be careful, Ms. Savannah," she said softly. She walked away from the table, and seconds later Gordon was sitting across from me.

"What did that old biddy want?" He glared at Beryl's back.

"Oh, you don't want to know." I faked a laugh, feeling slightly uneasy. Why did he make me feel uncomfortable? He was my friend. A supportive person I'd met in this small town. I needed friends, and I needed to stop being so suspicious.

"I probably don't." He laughed and picked up a menu. "Let's see what they have. I'm starving."

"Oh, yeah?"

"Yeah, I missed breakfast." He nodded and then leaned forward. "So, heard anything from Wade? He's not back already, is he?"

"No, he's still out of town."

"Okay, so where did he go? Was it for business? Fun?" He paused and then chuckled. "I sound like the FBI, don't I? Sorry for grilling you. Sometimes I get a bit intense. I guess it's the thespian in me."

"Yeah, that must be it." I smiled and I looked over to the counter to see Beryl staring at me with a blank expression on her face. She was starting to get on my nerves. If she had something she really needed to get off of her chest, then why didn't she just tell me? Who did she think she was? The head of the CIA or something?

"So, what's new with you?" Gordon asked.

I just shook my head. "About the same as last week." As much as I liked Gordon, I didn't want to tell him about me and Wade. It felt too special to talk about, at least with people I didn't really know. Plus I didn't want Gordon judging me. "What about you?"

"Not much." He looked down and I could see that he appeared nervous.

"Where did you end up going?"

"Going?" He looked up with a frown. "What do you mean?"

"I mean last week when I'd text you, didn't you say you

were out of town?"

"I don't remember." He looked around. "Waitress, can we order, please? We're hungry." He looked back at me and rolled his eyes. "You just can't get good service these days, can you?"

"You just got here, so it's not that bad," I said lightly, wondering when he'd become so entitled and rude. Had he always been like this?

"I know." He gave me a rueful smile. "Sorry, I've just had a lot on my mind recently." His expression had turned thoughtful and the light in his eyes had dimmed.

"Are you okay?"

"Am I okay?" He repeated my question and just sort of sat there as if he didn't know how to answer. And then within a few seconds, a bright smile spread across his face and he nodded. "Of course, I'm okay, why wouldn't I be?" He reached over and touched my hand lightly. "Thanks for asking, though. What about you? How's it been going with the Wolf of Herne Hill? Has he gotten his claws into you yet?"

"The wolf?" I laughed, hoping to change the subject. "Why do you call him the wolf?"

"Most probably because he likes to eat—"

"What would you like to order today?" Beryl interrupted his sentence and I was glad for it. I was pretty sure that if Gordon continued with his line of conversation that my face would give away the fact that Wade was now much more than just my boss.

"Lasagna?" I asked only half-jokingly.

Her eyelid didn't so much as twitch. "We have burgers today."

"Maybe I'll have a grilled cheese," I said with another smile and then suddenly it dawned on me: white bread, butter, and cheese. Those are the makings of a grilled cheese sandwich. Wade wanted me to make him grilled cheese? He hadn't acted like he was a huge fan when we were eating them in this very diner. But why then had he created a grocery list for the same ingredients?

"No grilled cheese today." Beryl looked at me then. "We're all out."

"Oh, okay. Then just a burger." I sat back and looked at my phone, hoping to see a call or message from Wade, but there was nothing. Where was he?

"Expecting a call?" Gordon looked down at my phone.

"Not really. My friend Lucy's coming to stay, so just thought she might text me or something."

"Oh, so you'll have some company." Beryl suddenly smiled. "That's good, very good." And then she walked away. I looked over at Gordon who had a small smile on his face, and I could see that he was trying not to laugh.

"What's so funny?"

"I don't think that lady likes me much." He rolled his eyes. "Nosey old busy body. Old people are always in everyone's business."

"I think she means well." I found myself growing prickly on Beryl's behalf. It wasn't like she'd even said anything about Gordon to me. It was Wade and his brother she'd been warning me about. She definitely seemed to have some sort of dislike for the Hart men.

"Yeah, people always say they mean well." He rolled his eyes. "Usually they only mean well when it benefits them in some way."

"You sound cynical."

"Nah." He shook his head. "Not more than most, anyway." And then he sat back and laughed. "Well, I'm a struggling actor, I guess I'm allowed to be a little cynical."

"I guess so." And then I really looked at him, as if really seeing him for the first time. His bright eyes glittered with an inner turmoil and the smile on his face seemed forced. "How is that, by the way? I suppose it takes a toll on you? Trying to make it in such a competitive field."

"Do you want the honest answer?" He half-smiled. "Or the one I give to people that don't know how to deal with the truth?"

"The honest answer." But even as I said it, I knew I was half lying. It was hard hearing about people's struggles. It was hard hearing about people's hurt and it was hard to know how to respond. I wanted the truth, but I also knew that it could be very painful to hear.

"I feel like a loser." There was no smile on his face now. "My whole life, I've never felt quite good enough, and now …" He looked out of the window for a few seconds. "There's nothing like not making it to confirm that what you've thought your whole life is true."

"You're not a loser, though. You're so talented." I leaned forward and squeezed his hand. "I've seen you perform and I wouldn't lie to you. You're really talented."

"Thank you." He looked back at me, his green eyes shining, and I wondered if he was close to tears. "I don't tell many people this, but I suffer from depression. I guess it goes back to my childhood." He shrugged. "There are some days that are so dark that I can't get out of my head, and I just want to be anywhere but here."

"Here as in Herne Hill Village?"

"Here as in my own body." He tapped his fingers against the table. "I guess I've always been searching, hoping, wanting more." Suddenly he stopped and his eyes sought mine, searching and connecting. I stared back at him, feeling the emotions pass through us. "You've got a kind soul, Savannah. You're a warm person. You don't deserve to be messed up in this."

"Messed up in what?" I smiled. "You're my friend and

I'm here for you, Gordon."

"I know." He chewed on his lower lip. "I just don't want you to think …" His voice trailed off and he took a deep breath. "Man, I'm hungry. Where's this food?"

"They can be a little slow here." I grinned. "The first time I came here with Wade, I was wondering if I was in the Twilight Zone." I laughed. "I asked for lasagna, ordered a burger, and was served a grilled cheese."

"Oh shit, that means today we get pickled herrings or something."

"Eww, gross!"

"Not if you're Scandinavian. They love that stuff."

"It's a good thing I'm not then, isn't it?" I grinned. "Though I think Lucy, my best friend, has some Swedish in her. I'm so excited for you to meet, Lucy. I think you'll get on really well."

"Wade's okay with her coming?"

"He doesn't know."

"Oh." Gordon's smile widened. "What the captain doesn't know can't hurt him, huh?"

"Captain?" I laughed. "I guess he does think he's the captain of his ship, doesn't he?"

"Yes, he does." Gordon spoke with so much knowledge that suddenly it struck me that he seemed to have a lot of opinions about someone he'd never even met. And once again a sense of foreboding hit me.

I shivered as I looked down at the table, repressing the urge to scream. How the hell had I found myself in some sort of scary thriller type situation? I was the romantic comedy girl. You couldn't pay me to watch a horror movie and yet, here I was, in the middle of some sort of low-budget Lifetime movie, and I was as clueless as all of the heroines.

I truly had no idea who in my life was good and who was bad.

CHAPTER 4

"Welcome to the Hart house." I held my hands up in the air as Gordon got out of his car and walked towards me. It was silly to sound so proud, as if it were my house, but for some reason I wanted Gordon to like it.

"Amazing. It's big, isn't it?" Gordon looked around. "Though I'd expect nothing different from Wade Hart. It must be grand to be him."

"Indeed it must." I nodded and walked toward the door. "Come in and I'll give you a tour."

As I opened the front door, my phone beeped. I waited for Gordon to walk inside before I checked it and my heart leaped when I saw Wade's name on the screen. So he was still alive, was he? I wanted to put the phone back in my handbag. I wanted to ignore him and let him sweat. Let him feel how angry I was. Maybe my feelings would drift through the air to him as if through osmosis.

"That's not osmosis," I chided myself under my breath. But then I smiled, not because I was happy but because Wade had texted me. He hadn't forgotten me. He wasn't ignoring me. He had thought about me and he had texted me. That had to mean something, right?

I knew what Lucy would say. I knew what I would say if it were Lucy in my position and I was giving her advice. I'd tell her that one simple text meant nothing. Actions spoke louder than idle texts. But, of course, that didn't stop the butterflies or the hope that surged through me. He'd texted and even though I was still pissed as hell at him, I was now feeling just a little bit less anxious. I would let him wait until I was ready to respond.

I had the patience of a flea though, and before I could stop myself, my fingers were flying across the keyboard.

"I'm hanging out. What's up?" Did that sound cool, calm, and collected? Did it sound like I couldn't care less that he had left me the morning after taking my virginity? Did it sound as though I didn't think he was a pig?

"Hanging out?" His reply text came back right away. "With whom and where?"

I stared at his response and smiled to myself. *Yeah, I think I'll let you wait for a further response from me, Wade Hart.* I followed Gordon into the house and ignored the twinge of guilt that I felt. This wasn't my house and I hadn't even asked Wade if I could have people over. I didn't think Gordon would trash the place or anything, but it almost felt like I was invading Wade's privacy by letting other people inside.

"This place is absolutely amazing." Gordon walked down the hallway, his fingers grazing the wall. "Man, everything must have cost so much money. I wonder how much Wade is worth?"

"I have no idea. I would assume he's a millionaire, though."

"I bet he's a billionaire." Gordon murmured. "I bet he's

the richest man in Herne Hill Village. I wonder if he has a safe in here."

"Why?" Nerves hit my stomach again.

"Just curious. I bet he does have a safe hidden in here somewhere with millions of dollars in cash. And I bet he has a secret hiding spot, one of those panic rooms."

"I don't know. He hasn't told me about either of those things."

"What would you do if you had a million dollars?" he asked me as he stopped to stare at what I believed to be an original Rembrandt painting.

"If I had a million dollars, I'd buy a house and a car and go on vacation." I paused for a few seconds. "Though, I'm not sure a million dollars would buy me a house in Manhattan. I'd have to move to New Jersey or something."

"Or you could come upstate." He grinned. "You could move to Westchester."

"That sounds like my worst nightmare." I laughed. "So okay, maybe I won't buy a house. Maybe I'll buy a two-bedroom apartment in Brooklyn for me and my best friend to live in."

"That sounds nice."

I turned towards the library, Gordon following closely behind me. "What would you do if you had a million dollars?" I asked over my shoulder.

"I've thought about that often." His voice was soft now. "I think I'd invest in some decent camera equipment and make a film."

"Oh, yeah? My friend Lucy wants to make films as well." I looked back at him. "I thought you wanted to act."

"I do." He grinned. "But I want to do it all. I want to write, act, direct, produce, edit. I want to win an Oscar, an Emmy, a Tony, a Nobel Peace Prize." He laughed. "I want everyone in the world to know my name and to love my work."

"I know you can do it. You can do anything you set your mind to. Plus you have the talent. You're definitely going to be a star one day, Gordon."

"Thanks! All I need is the money now." He sounded wistful. "Did I ever tell you that my dad was rich?"

"No, that's awesome. Wouldn't he lend you some money or back you?"

"No." He sounded bitter. "As far as he's concerned, I don't even exist."

"Oh, I'm sorry."

"I only know what he looks like because he's had his photo in the papers."

"Oh no, really?"

"I can't remember ever meeting him in real life. I can't remember even having a conversation with him. It's like I didn't exist in his world. I was nothing." His voice echoed down the hall. "Wow, I see why you love this room. Look at all this natural light and wow, the books." He stared around the library and I watched him, my heart aching for him.

"Why didn't your dad ever talk to you?" I asked him softly as my phone beeped again. I knew it was Wade without even looking and I ignored it.

"I guess because he didn't care." He shrugged. "He didn't want me. I was nothing in his life."

"But still he should have been there …" My voice trailed off as he walked to the window that looked out to the forest behind us.

"He was married. He had his 'legitimate' kids. I was nothing but the bastard."

"The bastard …"

I'd heard those words before. Hadn't Louisa, Wade's mom,

said that her husband had cheated on her and gotten another woman pregnant? Hadn't that been the reason why she'd said she'd left? I looked over at Gordon, and as he turned his face to the side and I studied his profile, a jolt of recognition hit me.

Was Gordon a Hart? Was he in fact Wade's brother?

"Gordon, can I ask you something?" The words barely left my mouth and then I heard a large creaking from the door as if someone had opened it. The hairs on the back of my neck stood up as if someone were behind me and staring at me. I turned to look at the doorway, but there was no one there. I walked over to it quickly and looked down the corridor, but it was empty.

"What did you want to ask me?" Gordon asked as he walked over to the bookshelves and started fumbling through the books.

"Uhm …" I felt hesitant to ask him what I was thinking now. If he was Wade's illegitimate brother, why hadn't he told me already? "I was just curious if you had any fun plans for the summer?"

"Oh, hmm, not really." He shook his head. "So, did I tell you that I met Wade's last assistant in the village as well?" He spoke idly. "She was a real looker, tall and blonde. Did Wade ever mention her to you?"

"No." I swallowed hard, not wanting to think about Wade being close with another woman. I was about to ask Gordon what he knew about her when he suddenly made a face.

"Where's the bathroom, please?"

"Oh, go down the hallway, last door on the right," I said and watched as he walked out of the room. I waited for a couple of seconds and then pulled my phone out of my bag again to see a few more messages from Wade.

"Are you still alive?"

"Have you run off with my millions and headed back to the City?"

"Savannah, where are you?"

I smiled at the texts and then responded. "Hey, I'm still here in Herne Hill, where exactly are you?"

"I told you I had to go away."

"Okay then, can I help you?"

"You sound cold."

"I didn't realize texts could sound cold."

"Where are you?"

"Why do you care?"

"Just wondering if you're thinking of me."

"Not."

"Are you mad at me?"

"What do you think?"

"Last night was special."

"Bye."

"Savannah …"

I was about to text him back when I heard a door slam. I frowned. Leaving the library, I headed for the kitchen.

"Gordon?" I said as I stopped outside the guest bathroom. There was no response. I said his name again, this time louder. "Gordon?"

"Hey, sorry." Gordon's voice sounded manic as he came out from a room across the hall. He'd been in Wade's office.

"What were you doing in there?"

"I got lost. Sorry. There are so many rooms in this place." He gave me a wry smile, but I found it hard to smile back. I walked over to Wade's office to close the door. As I peeked inside, I saw a piece of paper lying on the ground. Had Gordon been going through Wade's stuff? I wanted to confront him, but it made me too nervous.

"Hey, I just got a text from Lucy. There are some things she wants me to get from the store before I pick her and

Jolene up, so I think I have to cut our time short here. Sorry about that."

"Oh, man." He frowned. "I could wait here for you to get back?"

"No, I don't think so." I shook my head. "We should leave now."

"Are you mad that I got lost?" He gave me what I assumed was his puppy dog face, and I tried not to roll my eyes. Did he think I was stupid? Or that I was interested in him? And wasn't he gay? Why would he think I'd fall for that?

Because he's an actor, a voice in my head shouted at me. I wanted to slap myself. How had I been so blind as to everything that was going on around me?

"Do we have time to have a ..." Gordon started and his voice trailed off as I gave him my best death stare. I knew that he was slightly confused as to why I was being so cold to him, but I was done with men like him and Wade. Shit, for all I knew they were cut from the same cloth.

"It was great seeing you. Let's chat soon." I said as I closed the front door behind me and walked to my car. "Bye." I got into the car and slammed the door shut. I watched as Gordon got into his car. No way was I going to leave while he was still on the property. Who knew what he would do if I just left?

I started my car as soon as I saw his car driving away from the house and followed him out. As I pulled into the main road, I looked left and then right and was surprised that I couldn't see the tail of Gordon's car. He must have been driving fast to have made it out of sight already.

As I drove along the street, I wondered why he would have sped away.

CHAPTER 5

"Jolene, my darkling!" I bent down as my scrappy little dog came running towards me, tongue out.

"Did you just call her your darkling or your darling?" Lucy followed behind him at a much more leisurely pace. She was carrying two big duffel bags and Jolene's leash in her hands.

"I meant to say darling, but I called him darkling by mistake." I laughed as I rubbed the top of her head.

"Called *him* darkling?" Lucy raised an eyebrow. "Are you distracted or something?"

"Oh, oops." I kissed Jolene. "I meant her, my beautiful darling girl." I grinned and then gave Lucy a hug. "I'm so happy to see you. My mind has been all over the place."

"Thinking about Wade?"

"Who else?" I groaned as we talked towards the car. "I'm so glad you guys are here, though. I've missed you both so much. I don't even know how I've survived this long without you both."

"I don't know either, darkling." Lucy giggled and then

brought me in for a big hug. "I've missed you like, whoa! Also, Jolene may very well be related to the Dark Lord."

"The Dark Lord?"

"He who shall not be named." She giggled. "Sometimes I think Jolene was channeling him in the middle of the night when she would start whining to go out to pee."

"Oh no. I'm so sorry." I grabbed her bags to walk them the rest of the way to the car. "I owe you big time."

"I wouldn't say big time, but I want to know everything. *Everything*." She wiggled her eyebrows at me as we got to the Range Rover. "Nice ride."

"Well, my boss is kind of a big deal." I giggled as we got into the SUV. "Or at least he has a lot of money."

"I wouldn't mind him dropping me off a few stacks."

"Dropping you off a few stacks?" I raised an eyebrow as I pressed the button to start the engine. "Say what?"

"That's what all the cool kids say."

"We're not cool."

"I know, but we can try to be." She sat back in the seat and started messing with the buttons that operated the seat. "Oh shit, this seat has a massager and heats up?" She moaned as she sat back. "Can this be my new home?"

"Oh, Lucy, I've missed you." I laughed as I drove out of the parking lot and made the way back to Hart Manor (as I thought of it in my head). There's something about being with close friends that can just make your day. It's comforting and warm, and they make you feel secure and whole. Lucy was that friend for me. No matter how crazy my brain was or how fried my emotions were, when I was with Lucy, I felt a sense of peace and calm. "Thanks for coming, Luce, you truly are the best friend a girl could ask for."

"I learned from the best." She smiled at me and I grinned as I turned the radio on loudly. Top 40 music pumped out of the stereo and *I Hope* by Gabby Barrett started playing.

"I love this song." Lucy sang along to the radio and soon both of our voices were screeching into the wind. I looked in my rearview mirror and saw that Jolene had her out the window and was looking around eagerly. I realized this was the first time she'd ever been out of the city.

"Welcome to the country, Jolene." I laughed to myself at the irony. If anyone should have known the country, it was Jolene. Well, at least Dolly Parton's Jolene. "She's hypnotized by the trees."

"She's trying to think of all the different ways she can pee on them." Lucy rolled her eyes. "She'd climb them if she could."

"Haha, I bet she would."

"So tell me everything there is to know about Wade Hart." She peered at me as if trying to see into my soul. "You don't look any different."

"Should I?"

"In books, they always say that once a woman has lost her virginity, she has a glow and everyone around her seems to know. Frankly, you look just the same to me. I see no glow."

"Wait until tonight." I laughed. "I'll put on some fake tan and bronzer."

"You are a goof, Savannah." Lucy turned to look back out the window. "I know you said it was country out here, but man, there are no skyscrapers in sight. It's all trees and farmland."

"Do you hate it?"

"I don't hate it." She shook her head. "It's just different. I've been in New York too long. It's strange not staring out of the window and watching a homeless man cuss someone out or a taxi almost get in an accident."

"Oh, you make me miss the city far too much." I laughed

and then as we pulled into the long driveway, I turned to her. "This is Wade Hart Manor."

"Is that really the name?"

"No," I laughed. "But it should be. The way he goes on, you'd think he was some sort of nobility."

"You don't think he is, do you?"

"What?" I stopped the car and got out.

"Do you think he could be a prince or something?" Lucy walked up to the house, her eyes wide in awe. "Holy shit, he is really rich, isn't he?"

"Yes, he's rich, and no, I do not think he's a prince." I grabbed Jolene from the back seat.

"What about a duke or a lord?" She turned back to look at me. "Or maybe he was part of the Russian dynasty that had to flee after Stalin took over."

"I don't think so." I shook my head. "Though that would be kinda cool."

"You might have slept with one of the descendants of Louis XIV!"

"Hmm…" I cocked my head. "Louis XIV?"

"Off with their heads and let them eat cake." Lucy giggled. "I think those two quotes were from that time period, right?"

"You mean during the French Revolution? I think it was Marie Antoinette that said, 'let them eat cake,' and that was why she was beheaded. Well, that and many other reasons. Also, she was French, not Russian."

"Listen to you, Ms. Francophile."

"Hardly." I walked up to the front door and unlocked it. "Come on, let me show you inside."

"I can't wait." Lucy followed behind me into the foyer, and I let Jolene down onto the cool marble. She immediately started darting back and forth in excitement and I watched in horror as she slid along the marble into the wall and bumped her nose. She let out a small yelp and then went running down the hallway.

"Looks like Jolene already feels at home in her palace," Lucy observed.

"Oh God, Jolene, don't start feeling too at home!" I cried out, visions of poop and pee all over the place. I could just imagine Wade coming home to that hot mess. There was no way I could talk my way out of that.

"Oh, guess what, Savannah?" Lucy turned to me with a huge smile as we walked into the kitchen.

"What's that?" I asked her, my eyes sweeping the room and noticing the open French doors. Hadn't I locked them before I left? I briefly remembered walking back into the house after I'd been looking for Wade and closing the doors, but maybe I hadn't locked them properly. Or maybe Gordon had gone outside?

"I'm going to try out for a singing show."

"You're what?" My jaw dropped as I gave Lucy my full attention. I studied her face to see if she was joking. Please God, let her be joking.

"I was thinking of trying out for *The Voice* or even *American Idol*."

"Yeah, and I'm going to try out for America's Best Dancer. You've got to be kidding right?" I started doing the Robot and giggled. "You can sing as well as I can dance, which isn't saying much. Girl, I hate to burst your bubble, but you can't carry a tune."

"And you can't dance," Lucy sang in a high voice and started laughing. "I'm not joking though." She made a face. "I'm actually 100% serious."

"Oh God, Lucy, why?"

"Oh, I know I can't sing." She laughed. "But wouldn't that make a great documentary?"

"What? The tale of the girl who can't sing?" I wondered if my best friend had gone crazy.

"No, a story of someone so desperate to make it that they enter television contests just to get noticed."

"Hmm." I walked over to the fridge. "Do you want a drink?"

"I'd love a glass of white wine if you have any."

"Not red?" I asked in surprise. Lucy and I loved red wine more than anything in the world.

"White wine feels more classy, and this has to be the classiest house I've ever been in." Lucy twirled around the room. "I feel like I should be in a white dress with a huge skirt singing."

"What?" I laughed at the image in my mind.

"Or maybe in a maid's outfit."

"Girl, don't get me started on maid's outfits," I grumbled. "I can't believe Wade made me wear one."

"I bet he just wants you to wear it in bed. I bet he has some sort of boss fantasy and he wants to bend you over his desk and pull your garters down."

"Lucy, you've been watching too much porn."

"Not porn, actually," she sniffed. "French and Italian films. They are so much more open to sexuality than we are in France and Italy."

"So they have a lot of mainstream movies about bosses fucking their maids?"

"Savannah, watch your language please." She held her hand up. "I might have to take my belt off and give you a spanking."

"Yes, Wade-I-mean-Lucy." I rolled my eyes at her. "Is this your way of telling me that you're now a dominatrix?"

"No, but wouldn't that make a fantastic documentary … from Suburbia to the Dungeons … How I Became the Number One Dominatrix in the World?"

"Oh Lucy, stop, I can't …" I laughed so loudly that Jolene ran up to me and jumped up on my leg eagerly, hoping to join in whatever fun she thought she was missing. "Jolene, stop." I giggled and then I looked over at Lucy with a grateful smile on my face. "Girl, I am so glad you're here. You have really gotten my mind off of the whole Wade thing. It has been driving me crazy. I needed a good laugh."

"And that's why I'm here." She paused. "Well, that's not the only reason why I'm here. I also want us to figure out what's going on with Wade. We can be like Cagney and Lacey."

"Who?" I blinked at her.

"Come on, girl, *Cagney and Lacey*!" She huffed. "It's an old TV show, but it's still great."

"I'll take your word for it."

"Okay, we can be like Holmes and Watson."

"I'm Holmes." I grinned. "You can be Watson."

"How about I'll be Batman and you can be Robin?"

"I'll be Catwoman."

"I knew you were into tight lycra and whips." Lucy winked.

"Are you hungry?"

"A little. What happened to that wine you promised me?"

"Why don't we walk Jolene real quick and then come back and relax?" I looked at the clock. "Then we can watch a movie and gossip?" I headed towards the French doors and frowned when I noticed sprinkles of dirt on the floor. "Why is there mud inside?" I murmured.

"What's wrong, Savannah?" Lucy came up behind me. "I don't mind walking Jolene first and then coming inside."

"Nothing. I thought I'd closed this door, but maybe I was wrong." I stared at the ground. "Gordon was here earlier, and I guess that he went outside and trekked some mud in when he came back inside." I shrugged. "I like him as a person, but for some reason, I just don't trust him. I think he has some sort of ulterior motive for hanging out with me."

"Who are these men you know and why are they all shady?" Lucy sighed. "Sometimes, I'm happy I'm single, but then I go to bed at night all alone and wish I had someone."

"I know." I rubbed the back of her shoulders. "I'm in the same boat. I wish I had someone as well. And let's not say I do. I hardly think I have Wade Hart. Yes, I slept with him, but I don't think that really means much."

"Let's not give up hope, Savannah. Maybe he really is your knight in shining armor and we just don't know it."

"Yeah, maybe." I looked out the window and searched the sky. "I'm not seeing any flying pigs though, so maybe it's not my day for miracles."

"Oh, Savannah, come on, let's take Jolene out and you can show me the grounds to your mansion and then we can come back inside and snoop up a storm."

"I don't know about snooping." I bit my lip. "I was going to tell you later, but I think I caught Gordon snooping earlier."

"Oh, no way! Where? In your underwear drawer?" Her eyes widened. "He wants a piece of you as well?"

"No." I shook my head. "He was in Wade's office. He said he was in there by mistake, but I saw a piece of the paper on the ground." I pursed my lips. "He must have been going through his paperwork."

"But why would he be doing that?"

"I know this might sound crazy, but I think Gordon might be Wade's brother."

"Whaaaaaaaat?" Lucy looked shocked. "Shit, this is better than any movie. Why do you think they're brothers?"

"Well, I just have this feeling. Wade's mom told me that her husband had an affair, which resulted in a pregnancy. I know for a fact that the child wasn't in his father's life because Wade didn't even seem to know his dad had cheated."

"And the dad never said anything? Wow."

"Yeah. And Gordon keeps talking about his father who wanted nothing to do with him."

"Oh, shit. So you think he wants to get to know his dad now?"

"I doubt it. His dad is dead." I wrinkled my nose. "It's all so sad and sordid, really."

"Yeah, wow. What do you think Gordon is looking for?"

"No idea." I shook my head. "But if he is Wade's brother, it makes me wonder if any part of our friendship was real or if he was just using me."

"Oh shit, yeah. Ugh, that sucks."

"It does, but I feel bad for him. His father sucked. From what Louisa told me—she's Wade's mom—the dad was a real narcissist and only really cared about himself. It's just sad all around."

"You're a good person, Savannah, but don't let their family drama bring you down." Lucy looked thoughtful. "Do you think Wade's words had anything to do with Gordon? Maybe he knows that Gordon is his brother and doesn't want to share the inheritance with him and he thinks you might help Gordon get some of the money."

"You're smart, Lucy. I'd never thought of that, but you could be correct. All Gordon keeps talking about is money. Maybe that's why he was here. Maybe he was looking to help himself to what he thinks is rightfully his."

"Oh, man. I don't like this, Savannah." Lucy shook her head. "I don't like this at all."

CHAPTER 6

"Jolene is absolutely loving being able to run in the grass."
Lucy smiled as Jolene wiggled her ass into the ground and
then jumped back up and went running. "She loves it here."

"Yeah, she does, but I suppose there's a lot to love if
you're a dog."

"So, do you like it here?" Lucy's voice was suddenly
serious and the air between us felt tense.

Neither of us was comfortable being serious. I suppose it
was a defense mechanism that we'd developed growing up
with domineering parents. We both resorted to laughter and
goofing off, and while we always had each other's backs and
could tell each other anything, we seldom had deep conver-
sations.

"Surprisingly, I do," I replied.

"It seems like it would be lonely."

Jolene scampered off into the woods and we followed. I
shivered a little at the sudden coolness. The dense branches
above us blocked out most of the remaining sunlight.

"To be honest, I never felt lonely until today. When
Wade left." I reached my hands up and touched the lower

hanging leaves. "Of course, I missed you and wished you were here, but I didn't miss the city as much as I thought I would."

"I guess that's what happens when you meet someone who captures your heart."

"I suppose so."

"I've missed you, you know." Lucy sounded nostalgic. "But it also felt surprisingly freeing to be in the apartment by myself. Almost like I was a real functioning adult. I only had myself and it made me feel proud."

"So you didn't miss me at all, then?" I teased her, but a part of me was sad at what she'd said. Both of us were changing. We were growing up, becoming women instead of girls, and it scared the hell out of me.

"Of course I missed you!" She laughed. "It's not fun watching TV alone or eating alone, or even walking to the bar alone." She looked over at me. "I know it's good for us to grow up, but I'm not ready for our lives to go in separate directions."

"Neither am I."

"So what's it like living with Wade? You make him sound like such an asshole, but I know that there has to be something positive to him. If you fell for him and slept with him, there has to be something more."

"He makes me feel alive in a way that I never knew was possible. All these years I've been living, but I've never really been *living*, you know? He makes me enjoy mundane activities, he makes me feel happy to breathe the air. Everything seems so much grander, so much better. Even sparring with him makes me feel as if I'm floating through the sky. It's kinda crazy the way he makes me feel. I must be crazy for still being here after all the weirdness that's going on."

"It sounds amazing." Lucy's voice was wistful. "I want a man that makes me feel alive."

"Don't forget the crazy part as well." I laughed.

"It reminds me of that quote from *Rebecca* by Daphne du Maurier. Let me think, how did it go again? 'It wouldn't make for sanity, would it, living with the devil.' Yes, that was it."

"Oh, I don't remember that one, but yes, it's true. You know which quote from Rebecca springs to my mind?"

"No, tell me."

"'If only there could be an invention that bottled up a memory, like scent. And it never faded, and it never got stale. And then, when one wanted it, the bottle could be uncorked, and it would be like living the moment all over again.'" I walked along the pathway as I quoted from the book. "I understand now. I understand why some people want to stop time or bottle a memory. That night with him. The way he touched me, the way he kissed me, the feeling of him inside of me, it was magic. I never wanted it to end. I could have died with him in me and been in bliss."

"Oh, Savannah, you're so far gone, aren't you?"

"So far."

"We need to figure out what's going on. I don't want you madly and deeply in love with a bad man."

I stopped short and turned to her. "Oh, Lucy, what if he's a bad man? What if he's a really bad man?"

"Then you'll leave with me." Her voice was firm. "I know you're being all romantic and sappy now, but there's no way on God's green earth that I'm leaving you with a psycho."

"What if I won't go?"

"I'll pick you up, kicking and screaming."

"You really are good people, aren't you, Lucy?"

"Nah, I'm just your best friend. You'd do the same for me."

"I would." I caught my breath and looked around for Jolene. "Jolene, come on girl, let's go back inside."

Jolene was ahead of us, sniffing at something in the trees. I whistled for her. Beside me, Lucy stretched. I could tell that she was tired. I had a feeling that we wouldn't be having wine tonight, but that was okay. We always had tomorrow.

"Jolene, come now!" I called again, my voice firmer this time. "We're going back inside." Jolene looked up, her expression disappointed as she reluctantly walked back to me. I bent down to rub her between the ears as she reached me and then froze as I heard the sound of branches snapping. I looked up at Lucy. "Did you hear that?"

Lucy nodded, looking a little nervous. "Are there bears in these woods?"

"Girl, I have no idea." I put my fingers to my lips to tell her to be quiet and we listened some more. I heard the sound of more snapping branches and then a loud bang.

"What the hell was that?" Lucy's eyes were wide and I could feel all the blood leaving my face.

"I have no idea, but we need to go back inside now." I grabbed Jolene's leash and stood up. "Let's run."

Grabbing Lucy's arm with my free hand, I took off. I was exhausted, but fear kept me going, even as my legs trembled with fear.

CHAPTER 7

"Savannah, you know I love thrillers and scary movies, but this is too much!" Lucy was gasping as we ran back into the house. "What was that noise?"

"Maybe an animal in the woods?"

"An animal with a gun?" She raised an eyebrow. "I didn't know animals were packing now."

"It's their 2nd Amendment right," I joked. "The right to bear arms."

"This isn't funny, Savannah. This is getting creepier and creepier."

"I'm wondering if Gordon didn't come back here." I bit my lip. "Maybe he has something to do with everything that's been going on."

"You need to tell that psycho to leave you alone. I know you think he's a nice guy, but the things you've been telling me make me think he's not that great."

"Well, it's only recently that stuff has started to seem off to me. Are you tired or do you still want that wine?"

"I'm a little tired, but that running woke me up. Let's have some wine and do some research. Let's find out everything there is to know about Wade and Henry Hart." Lucy flopped dramatically into one of the kitchen chairs.

"Gordon was curious to know their net worth." I walked to the cupboard to grab some wine glasses. "He thinks they're billionaires."

"That doesn't shock me, but why would he care?" She paused. "I guess if he's their illegitimate brother, then he wants his share."

"Yeah, I mean I get it, I just wish he'd be honest about it."

"Why don't you just ask him?"

"You know I don't like confrontation."

"I know, but it's time to put your big girl pants on, Savannah. You didn't ask Wade about what you heard. You haven't asked Gordon why he's asking all these weird questions. You need to start being a bit more in these guys' faces. Don't let them think you're just some silly girl who'll believe whatever bullshit they flinging your way. Call them out on it, girl. You're strong, not afraid. Too many men think they can just do whatever they want and women will just accept it. That shit might have passed in the 1950s, but we're in 2020 now, and we're not going to put up with it."

"You're right, of course." I grimaced, still feeling a tinge of nerves at the possibility of having to ask Wade and Gordon what was really going on. "It's still scary to have to question someone, though."

"I know, girl, but you have nothing to be afraid of. If they don't like it, then they can lump it. And honestly, if you're scared that their answers will reveal that they're shitty men, then it's better to know now before you get even more involved with them."

"You're the voice of reason." I felt calmer just listening to her. "You know who you remind me of?"

"Mother Teresa?"

I laughed out loud. "You wish."

"Bella Hadid?"

"Who?"

"You know, that supermodel girl? Or maybe she's a super influencer?"

"Never heard of her, so no. And I should clarify it's a what, not a who."

"A what? I'm so confused."

"You remind me of self-help memes on Instagram. They always say something like, 'Tell him the truth and if he leaves, then it's on him.' Or 'Be your own flower and bloom.'" I grinned. "I'm getting the quotes wrong but you know what I mean."

"Yeah, I know what you mean. I guess that's good?"

"It's great! You're my own personal therapist."

"I wouldn't go that far, girl, but we're too smart to be weak and pathetic. I know you like Wade and I know you slept with him and that makes you feel like you're in love or whatever, but if he's an asshole, you're out of here. I will drag you out kicking and screaming if that's what it takes." She gave me her tough-guy look. "You're not going to be a statistic."

"He's not a serial killer, Luce."

"We don't know *what* he is. I've never even met him and I don't care one iota about him. If we find out any crap, I'm not letting you stay. Also, I'm not leaving until we figure it all out."

"And what if he comes back before then?" I hadn't antici-pated Lucy staying for more than a couple of days.

"And what?" Her eyes narrowed. "Girl, this place is crazy. I'm not leaving until I'm 100% sure you're safe. I'm not one of those people who just leaves their friend in danger and hopes it will work out."

"What about your job?"

"It's an internship." She shrugged. "I mean, it's a good internship and it pays, but it is what it is. I called my boss before I left to see if I could work from here for the time being. I don't really need to be in the office right now, so let's see what they say."

"What did I do to get a friend like you?" I swallowed, my throat suddenly thick with emotion. "You really are the best friend a girl could ask for, you know that?"

"I'm here for you, for life. And I'm never going to allow you to put up with shit or to be in harm's way. Never. What's that saying, we are our brother's keeper? I'm your keeper, girl. I am here for you. You can count on me for absolutely anything, at any time. You can tell me anything, I will always have your back. You're my best friend, Savannah. You're like a sister to me." Her voice caught. "I'm going to get emotional and I'm really not trying to, but all my life I prayed for a best friend like you. Someone who had my back. My ride or die, and you've been it. I know you have this attraction to Wade, and I know you want him to be a good guy. And I want that so badly for you. But if he's not a good guy, I'm going to be here to break your fall."

"Lucy, everyone deserves a best friend like you." I squeezed her hand. "And whichever lucky guy gets you is going to be the most blessed man in the world."

"I hope so." She smiled ruefully. "I can't seem to meet any guy that feels that way about me."

"All in good time." I smiled. "Trust me, I know he's out there for you. And you know what? If Wade is a shit head, I will leave with you." Even as I said the words, I felt a sharp pain in my gut. It would be hard to leave. It would be so damn hard.

"Come on, you grab the wine and I'll grab my laptop, and let's do some sleuthing."

"Don't you want to see your room first and have a shower?"

"Girl, if I have a shower, I'm going to sleep." She giggled. "Show me later."

"Okay." I grinned. "I understand." I pointed to the hallway. "Go down there, take the first right and you'll be in the living room. We can chillax on the sectional and see what we can find."

Lucy grabbed her bag and walked to the living room, Jolene trotting behind her. I felt a twinge of jealousy that my dog hadn't waited for me, but I knew that I was being irrational. I found a bottle opener and grabbed a bottle of zinfandel and carried them into the living room along with the wine glasses.

⚜

"Okay, girl, I found something interesting." Lucy looked up from her laptop as I handed her a very full glass of wine.

"Oh, what's that?" I sat next to her on the couch and leaned over to rub Jolene's ears before having a large sip of the chilled wine.

"So, Wade Hart is CEO of Hart Enterprises, right?"

"Yeah, that's the name of the company."

"And his dad was Joseph Hart?" Lucy sipped her wine, her eyes not leaving the screen.

"Yeah, the dad was Joseph and the mom is Louisa, or as I like to think of her, Queen Bitch."

Lucy laughed. "Okay, well did you know that a few years ago, the company was in really big trouble?"

"Oh God, what now? What happened?" I shook my head. "And no, I didn't know."

"They were on the verge of bankruptcy." Lucy was

reading quickly. "People thought it might have been the next Bernie Madoff case."

"Bernie Madoff, the guy that stole all those people money?" I raised an eyebrow. "No way."

"Yeah, he was being investigated by the SEC and some other government agencies. A number of his clients were concerned about how he was investing their money."

"Really?" I frowned. "I didn't know they had a hedge fund or anything. Wade doesn't seem to do anything like that." I tried to think about all the calls I'd been involved in. "He lends money to third world countries for development and some other corporate real estate stuff."

"Hmm, I don't know, but this reporter from the *New York Times* has several investigative articles on him."

"Oh, yeah? What's his name?"

"Not a him. A her. Her name is Misha Waterman."

"Oh, okay. So, what happened?"

"Well, from what I can tell, the company never filed for bankruptcy." She frowned. "Maybe I'll email this reporter and see what she has to say."

"Okay, but what does that have to do with me? Wade said he never should have hired me because I could ruin everything. What do I have to do with his dad nearly going bankrupt?" I sighed.

"Yeah, I don't know. Have you seen any files implicating Wade or Henry in any shady business dealings?"

"No." I shook my head. "I mean, we can have a peek in his office and see if we find any files." I suddenly remembered something. "Oh shit, Lucy, what if that was what Gordon was looking for? What if he's not the illegitimate son but a reporter?"

"Oooh, wow. Maybe." Lucy's eyes widened as she stared up at me. "Maybe that's why he was asking about Wade's net worth?"

"Yeah, but that doesn't really make sense now. Ugh, I need to talk to him."

"You really do." She took another sipped and moaned orgasmically. "This tastes so good. This is not Two-Buck Chuck from Trader Joe's."

I laughed. "I doubt Wade has ever even been in a Trader Joe's." I took a sip as well. "Okay, so I guess my first task is to try and talk to Gordon and then see what else we can find. There's a lady that works in the cafe in the village, she's always warning me about the Hart brothers. Maybe we can talk to her and see what she has to say."

"It can't hurt." Lucy tried unsuccessfully to suppress a yawn.

I jumped up and smiled at her. "Come on, sleepyhead. Let's get you to your room. I'm going to change the sheets while you shower."

"Oh?"

"I think it's best if you sleep in my room and I'll sleep in Wade's room." I smiled and then rolled my eyes as she made sex noises. "He's not there, so it's not like anything will be happening."

"I bet you wish it was, though."

"Maybe." I winked and then whistled at Jolene to get off of the couch. "Come on, you two." I headed toward the door. "Tonight, we all need to get a lot of sleep, and then tomorrow we can start afresh with this investigation."

"Sounds good to me." Lucy let out a bigger yawn. "Man, that's the problem with wine. It always accelerates how tired I feel."

"No worries, girl. We've already done a lot today, and I'm just so happy that you came up to visit me. I'm really looking forward to showing you around Herne Hill, and I can't wait for you to meet Wade."

"Trust me, girl, no one is more excited to meet this mystery boss of yours than I am."

Lucy linked arms with me and we sang one of our favorite Disney songs from *Beauty and the Beast* as we walked down the corridor. Just as we got to my room, an owl outside hooted. We both jumped and then laughed. Lucy headed to the bathroom and I started stripping the sheets so that I could change them.

The owl hooted again but this time, the sound sent a shiver through me. I walked over to the window and looked out but all that greeted me was the night sky and some stars. What was out there in the woods? Was someone trying to mess with my head or was I letting my imagination run away with me?

I didn't have the answers to those questions, but I did know that I was more thankful than I'd ever been in my life that Lucy had come to stay with me.

CHAPTER 8

Silence greeted me as I woke up the next morning. I snuggled under the sheets and pressed my face against Wade's pillow, breathing in his scent. I felt a little bit creepy doing it, but I loved the feeling of being close to him that it provided me. He wasn't here, but that was almost better. I could almost pretend that this was a normal situation and that Wade was a normal guy.

Almost.

And then, as if Wade could read my mind, my phone beeped with a text from him.

"Wakey wakey, sleepyhead."

I smiled at the text and a warm feeling spread through me. "How do you know I'm awake?" I typed back quickly then I stretched.

"Because you just texted me back."

"Wow, you're a regular Einstein."

"I'm the smartest man you know. Are you still in bed?"

"Why?"

"I just want to know if I should picture you with your hair all over the place or not."

"Not."

"Liar."

"Then why ask?"

"What are you wearing?"

"Don't you have work to do? Didn't you go away for business? Shouldn't you be concentrating on that?"

"I'd rather concentrate on making you come."

"Okay …"

"Are you touching yourself?"

"Are you?"

"Yes."

"Well, good for you."

"I'm touching myself thinking of you."

"I'm surprised you didn't want to video chat."

"Nah, not the best idea."

"Why not?" I frowned. Why didn't he want to see me and chat at the same time?

"Because that makes it feel cheap."

"Makes what feel cheap?"

"Phone sex."

"Oh, who's having phone sex?"

"Us."

"You wish."

"Don't you want to make my wishes come true?"

"Am I a genie?"

"You can be my genie in a bottle, anytime."

I giggled out loud at his messages.

"Savannah, you up?" Lucy pushed open the door and stuck her head inside the room. "Morning. I thought I heard you laughing."

"Wade was texting me." I sat up. "Come in." I waved her towards the bed. She was still in her nightgown, her hair loose and messy. "You're so pretty." I frowned playfully at her. "How do you make bedhead look so good?"

She laughed. "I look a hot mess, and you know it."

"No, you don't." I gave her a quick hug as she sat on the bed. Jolene jumped up onto the sheets as well and wiggled her way over to me for a rub down.

"So, what did Wade want?"

I felt my face get warm. "I don't think I should say."

She laughed, holding her hand out to me. "Okay, let me see the messages. I got to know how dirty his dirty talk is."

"Who said it was dirty talk?"

"Your red cheeks do." She sat back. "So, this is Wade's room?" She looked around. "It's nice."

"Yeah, it is. How did you sleep?"

"Like a log." Lucy stretched. "Your bed is so comfortable. I love it."

"Yeah, it's amazing. Want to have breakfast and a morning swim? Then we can go into town and chat with Beryl and see if we can get any more info on Wade."

"Sounds like a plan to me." She grinned. "Your phone is blowing up. Are you not going to answer your messages?"

"Wade can wait."

"Yes, he can." She laughed. "I bet he's ready to blow right now, though."

"What?"

"If I interrupted you while he was pleasuring himself, I bet he's on the way to blue balls." She giggled. "His hand is mid cock, wondering when it can start moving again."

"Lucy, you're disgusting."

"Am I, though?" She giggled as she slid off the bed. "I'm going to have a quick shower, then I'll make breakfast and we can have a swim."

"Sounds good." I nodded. "I'll get a shower now, too."

"Before or after you pleasure your man?"

"He's not my man, and I'm not having phone sex with him."

"But you want to, though!"

"Maybe." I giggled. "To be honest, I actually would prefer for him to be here and we have some fun in person." I winked. "That would really make my day."

Lucy groaned. "I'm officially jealous. Once we get back to the city, you're going to help me find a guy. I want a hottie who is going to make me come so hard that I forget my own name."

I laughed. "You sound hornier than me. But I will definitely help you find a guy. I want us both to end up with great guys, and if Wade turns out to be a dickhead, I'll be looking for a man for myself as well." I grimaced. "And let's be real, that's looking very likely."

"We'll see." Lucy grabbed Jolene off the bed. "Come on, girl, let's go and do a pee-pee before I shower." Jolene wagged her. I was a little jealous seeing how well they were getting on. They'd bonded a lot, and I could tell that Jolene loved Lucy just as much as she loved me now.

"You can leave her with me if you want."

Lucy shook her head. "You have your fun with Wade, and then I'll hand Jolene back over to you. I wouldn't want innocent little Jolene to witness something she shouldn't," she added primly.

Heat rushed to my face. "Lucy, you're ridiculous."

"Uh huh." She giggled and then started singing. "I don't see nothing wrong with a little bump and grind and phone sex in the morning."

"Lucy, out!" I screeched and threw a pillow at her. "I will meet you in the kitchen in thirty minutes. Have your swimsuit on."

"Yes, ma'am." She laughed. "Does Wade like it when you're bossy? Does he like a dominant woman?"

"Out!" I laughed and Lucy giggled her way out of the

J. S. COOPER

room. I grabbed the phone to see Wade's texts and smiled as I read them quickly.

"I was thinking that it would be nice to see you in some sexy lingerie. Order one online so that when I'm back you can model it for me."

"Did you order it yet?"

"Savannah, did you fall asleep again?"

"Are you pleasuring yourself thinking about me staring at you in your sexy outfit?"

"Savannah?"

"Are you really going to leave me hanging?"

"Or rather, I should say, are you really going to leave my dick hanging?"

"My hard dick."

"My hard dick that wants to be inside of you."

"Fuck, is your pussy as wet as I think it is right now?"

"I wish I was there to taste you. Slide my tongue into you and lick up your juices."

"Savannah, are you mad at me? Do you not like the dirty talk?"

"I can start over? How's your day going?"

"Planning on doing anything fun?"

"Savannah!!!"

I laughed at the exclamation marks at the end of his last text. I had to admit he'd made me horny. I wondered what it would feel like to be waking up to him going down on me. I was pretty sure it would feel amazing.

"Sorry, I was busy with my other man. He was just getting me off," I typed back.

"What other man, you tease? You deserve a spanking for that lie."

"Oh well, you're not here, so not going to happen."

"What were you doing?"

"Nothing."

"Another spanking for another lie."

"Whatever."

"Slip your fingers into your panties."

"I don't think so. I'm about to make breakfast and do some work. I still need to go through those files you left for me and type up those letters you wanted to send to the World Bank."

"I'm glad you're such a hard worker, but right now I have other things for you to do."

"Are you saying touching myself is now a part of my job description?"

"Do you want it to be?"

"You can't control when I touch myself."

"You want to bet?"

"You're so full of yourself. I have to go now."

"Minx."

"Bye, Wade, have a good day." I turned my phone off and then closed my eyes as I slipped my fingers into my panties and thought of him. I was horny as hell, but I didn't want him to know that. He had left me hanging, so I was going to do the same thing to him. That didn't mean I wasn't going to get mine, though. As my fingers touched my wetness, I imagined his tongue on me and my body shuddered with the sweet memory of my intimate times with him.

CHAPTER 9

"So, I could get used to this life." Lucy beamed as we pulled out of the driveway. "Yummy breakfast and a morning swim. What a life."

"Yeah, thanks for making that omelet. It was delicious."

"I don't even feel guilty for the Nutella on toast we had." Lucy laughed. "That morning swim worked off all the calories."

"I don't know about all the calories, but definitely a lot."

I turned on the radio and we both fell silent as we listened to the music. I drove slowly into town, my soul heavy with apprehension as we headed toward the cafe. I dreaded what we might find out.

"You okay, Savannah?" Lucy's voice broke into my thoughts.

"Sorry, what?"

"I just asked you the same question five times and you still haven't answered me."

I flashed her a wry smile. "My mind was occupied."

"It certainly seems that way." Lucy turned the radio

down. "I was asking if you knew the name of this song, but that doesn't matter. Why are you so tense?"

"I guess I'm just nervous to hear what Beryl is going to tell us about Wade. Like, if it's really bad, what do I do?"

"Girl, first of all, I don't think we're going to crack the case so easily. Whoever heard of a detective solving the case by speaking to one person? But if on the off-chance Beryl happens to be the Miss Marple of the village and is able to tell us absolutely everything and it's bad, then we leave."

"We just leave without giving Wade a chance to explain?"

"To explain what, girl? If he's an asshole, he doesn't get anything. He doesn't deserve you to give him a chance to explain."

"Well, but …"

"Girl, a little bit of loving hasn't turned you into a first-class fool has it?"

"No." I laughed, even though I didn't want to. "And just wait until you have sex. You won't be referring to it as *a little bit of loving*."

"Oh yeah, what will I be referring to it as?"

"A whole hunka hunka bit of loving." I giggled, suddenly feeling happier again.

"You know that doesn't even make sense right? What's a whole hunka hunka?"

"It means a whole lot."

"I don't think it does." Lucy shook her head. "Doesn't hunka hunka mean like hot or really attractive? Like a hot guy. Didn't Elvis Presley say it in his song, 'Burning Love'?"

I rolled my eyes. "I don't know. Are you the hunka hunka police?"

"I just might be." Lucy dropped into a deep Southern voice. "Let me just put on my blue suede shoes and I'll give it some thought."

"Ha ha ha." I turned onto the main road and was pleased

to realize that my nerves had subsided. "But you're right, I'm not going to make any decisions until I have all the facts."

"I don't actually think I said that, but whatever. Sounds like a good plan to me."

"Good!" I took a deep breath. "Okay, we're nearly there. Let's see what Beryl has to say."

❧

"**W**elcome to Herne Hill Village Cafe," Beryl greeted us as we walked in. "A table for two or will others be joining you?" She looked over at Lucy and studied her. "You're new in town, too?"

"Hi, I'm Lucy, Savannah's best friend. I just came up to ensure that all is well in the village and that Savannah is safe." Lucy held out her hand, but Beryl ignored it.

"Well, I'm glad to hear she has a good friend." Beryl nodded. "I don't like to see young girls do foolish things. They can get themselves in a whole heap of trouble, you know?" She turned a meaningful gaze on me.

"Actually, that's why we're here." I licked my lips nervously and lowered my voice. "I was hoping to talk to you today, Beryl. About Wade and the Hart men."

"Oh." She blinked once and then shrugged. "I don't really know what I can tell you, dear. I'm just a simple waitress in a cafe."

"Oh. I thought …" Beryl walked away before I could finish. I looked at Lucy, whose eyes were now narrowed. "Well, that was a fail. What are you thinking?"

"I'm thinking we need to go and sit at the counter and order some coffee and maybe some doughnuts. I feel like something sweet right now."

"But you heard her. She has nothing to say."

"Savannah, I love you, but you would make the absolute

worst detective in the history of detectives. It's *obvious* that she has something else to say. We're not just going to walk away."

"We're not?"

"Nope." She stepped in front of me. "Hey, Beryl, can we sit at the counter? We just want to order some coffee and maybe some pancakes or doughnuts."

Lucy marched to the counter and took a seat without waiting for Beryl's answer. I followed behind her like a puppy dog and sat next to her.

"I'll be with you in a moment," Beryl said. To my surprise, she was smiling as widely as I'd ever seen her.

I waited for her to be out of earshot before I whispered to Lucy. "Do you think this is a good idea?"

"Yes, of course. You know what I was thinking?" Lucy's eyes were wide as she leaned in towards me.

"What?"

"What if the house is haunted and Wade is actually a ghost?"

"What? What are you talking about?"

"All the weird things you've been experiencing in the house might be supernatural. And has anyone else ever seen Wade asides from you?"

"*Yes,* Lucy." I held back a laugh. "He and I were in here just a couple of weeks ago. Beryl and everyone else that was in here saw him."

"Are you sure they saw him? Did they talk to him or just to you?"

"Oh my God, why did my best friend have to be a film-maker?" I shook my head. "This isn't a Gothic horror movie. And if it is, I want out."

"How cool would that be, though?"

"I don't really think I want to have lost my virginity to a ghost, so not cool at all."

"Oh, yeah, I almost forgot you guys had sex." She laughed. "But maybe the house is haunted. Wouldn't that be cool? What happened to the last assistant, again? Maybe she's haunting the place to get revenge on Wade for killing her."

"Uhm … That's even worse. Now Wade has gone from a ghost to a murderer?"

"Well, I'm not saying he's a murderer, but let's be real, he's not worried you're going to find out he's secretly donating millions to feed the poor. Whatever he's hiding is dark. *Really* dark."

"Lucy, you're not helping."

"Sorry." She offered me a wry grin. "I'm just getting so many ideas for movies. I wish I'd brought my camera with me."

"You didn't bring it?"

"Well, I did." She laughed. "I just wasn't sure how you'd feel if I started taking some footage."

"Girl, do what you want. If you feel inspired, go for it."

"The woods are cool. Maybe we can go for a walk again this evening and I can take some shots. That would be pretty awesome."

"Yeah, sure, I don't mind." I shrugged. Frankly, that was the least of my concerns. She could take as many videos as she wanted. All I cared about was finding out what Wade was hiding. Also, I missed him, which made me feel stupid. I wanted to see his face. I wanted to hear his voice. I wanted to touch him. I even missed his teasing.

"So, ladies, what can I get you?" Beryl stopped in front of us. "Black coffees or do you want milk?"

"Coffees with milk," Lucy answered promptly. "And we want some answers. No games, please. I think you know something and you can help us. You're a good lady, Beryl. I know you care about my friend. And I care about her. So, let's do our best to ensure she gets the answers she needs before something bad happens to her. I know you don't want that on your conscience, do you, Beryl?"

Beryl was silent for a few moments staring at Lucy. Then she switched her gaze to me. "You have a good friend there."

"I know."

"Hold on … I'll put in your order for the eggs benedict, and I'll be back."

"I said doughnuts or pancakes—" Lucy started but I just shook my head at her.

"We'll have whatever you recommend, Beryl, thank you." I gave the older lady a small smile and sat back as she walked away. "That was awesome, Lucy, I think she's really going to give us some good information now."

"She'll give us something." Lucy shrugged. "Though I can tell you already that it won't even be a tenth of what she knows." She looked thoughtful. "Old ladies like that, that work in cafes like this? They see and hear everything." She nodded to herself. "Beryl knows a lot. She won't tell us everything, but she'll give us a hint, and that will be enough."

"How will that be enough?" I frowned. "Can't we try and get her to tell us everything?"

"We'd be here all day and night for a year if we tried that." She shook her head. "All we need are some crumbs. We can go from there."

"Where, though?"

"Gordon!" She raised an eyebrow. "And maybe we can go to the local library, see if we can find out any information there."

"I guess so."

"Also, you know who we didn't look up online yesterday?"

"Who?"

"We didn't look up his mom." Lucy tapped her fingernails against the countertop. "I feel like she has to know something as well."

"There's no way she would tell me. "She doesn't think I'm good enough for her son."

"Maybe that's precisely the reason that she *would* tell you." Lucy seemed to be in full-on detective mode. "If she feels the only way you would leave is to hear the bad stuff, maybe she'd be more than happy to fill you in."

"Hmm, I don't know. I feel like she would have told me already if that was the case. I told you that this lady cannot stand me."

"Most women don't like the girls their sons date, just like most dads don't like the guys their daughters date. It's that whole Oedipus thing."

"That's crazy."

"Crazy but true."

"Yeah, I guess …"

I was starting to feel overwhelmed again. Lucy was taking charge, which was nice, but she was almost pushing it too much. Yes, I wanted answers but was I willing to pay the price? I at least wanted to see Wade again before I found out something that might break my heart. I almost regretted telling Lucy everything. Part of me just wanted to live in denial for a little bit. Was ignorance really such a bad thing?

"Hey, ladies, here are your coffees." Beryl suddenly reappeared and put two slightly stained white coffee cups on the counter in front of us. "Sugar is in front of you. The French toast will be out soon."

"Great, thanks …" Lucy gave me a confused look.

"So, Beryl," I spoke up then because as much as I loved Lucy, I didn't want her taking over. I was a strong, capable woman. And I could handle the truth, even if it broke my heart. "You've been making comments and little insinuations to me about the Hart men since I came to Herne Hill. I would really appreciate it if you would tell me what you know. And if you think I'm in any sort of danger."

"You found your voice again, eh?" Beryl took a seat on the stool next to mine. "I don't have much to say. I'm just a simple woman that lives in the village and minds her own business."

"Yes, of course." I pressed my lips together to stop from laughing. If Beryl really thought she minded her own business, then she was as delusional as they came.

"But I hear things, working here," she continued. "About them Hart men. I mean, they pretty much own the town, or at least they did." She looked around for a few seconds as if checking to see if anyone was paying attention to us. "Look, all I'm going to say is that the Hart men are full of secrets." She said *secrets* in a low voice. "Them boys, well, let's just say there's more than one actor in that family. Those Harts have blood on their hands." She was getting more heated up now. "Everyone knows that the seeds can't be good if the core is bad."

"Uhm, okay." I blinked. "Could you please explain that a b—"

She suddenly slid off her stool. "That's all I'm going to say." She pursed her lips. "Ain't not a one of them a Cary Grant or Clint Eastwood, that's all I got to say."

And with that, she was gone again. I wanted to call after her, ask her to just talk in plain English and not in riddles, but I just kept my mouth shut.

"Well, that was majorly frustrating," I grumbled. "I can't believe—" I stopped speaking when I realized Lucy was scribbling something down on a piece of paper. "What are you writing?"

"I'm writing down what she said." Lucy's eyes were shining as she looked up at me. "She said that there are two actors in the family." Lucy was excited. "I think she just confirmed your suspicion that Gordon is a Hart brother! Isn't he an actor?"

"Yes …" And suddenly my heart was racing as well. "I didn't think of it like that, but yeah, he is an actor. I really don't think Wade or Henry are, though. You don't think they're secretly famous actors or something and haven't said anything?"

"No." Lucy shook her head. "You'd recognize a famous actor, even if you didn't know them well."

"True, especially with all the movies we watch."

"What's the definition of an actor?"

"Huh?"

"What's the def—"

"I know what you asked, I just don't know why you asked it."

"Let me search on my phone and see. So, when I go to Google there are two definitions. One is a person whose profession is acting on the stage, in movies, or on television. The second is a participant in an action or process."

"Okay, and what? Wade is going to be trying out for the next community theater play in the village?"

"No, no, I'm saying, what if she didn't use the term literally? Maybe she's not saying that the other brother is trying to make it big in Hollywood but rather is putting on an act or a front."

"Oh, hmm. So, Wade might be acting like he likes me when really he couldn't care less. Like a sociopath? Oh shit, do you think Wade is a sociopath?"

Lucy shook her head. "That's one way to look at it, but that's not what I was thinking. I'm just saying I think Beryl was alluding to some big lie, some big secret. That adds up to what you heard Wade saying."

"I know that Wade has a secret, though. That tells us nothing."

"The other thing that she said that I thought was quite interesting was that the Harts have blood on their hands ..."

"So, he's a murderer?"

"No." Lucy shook her head. "If he was a murderer, Beryl would have said. She wouldn't have let us stay there. I'm pretty sure." She didn't sound sure.

"Then what else could she have meant?"

"I don't know." Lucy shook her head. "And also, what does, 'the seeds can't be good if the core is bad' mean? Are they involved in any sort of farming or food manufacturing?"

"Not that I know of ..." I paused. "Well, actually, kind of. They're helping over countries with their farming practices." I tried to remember exactly what they were doing. "I'd have to check."

"Yeah, we can maybe check at the library. Why don't you try and give Gordon a call? I think we need to talk to him."

"Okay." I pulled my phone out and called him, but the call went directly to voice mail. "I think his phone is off. Let me text him and ask him to call me." I shot off a quick text.

Lucy and I locked eyes for a moment then shook our heads. I knew that she was thinking the same thing I was.

How deep into this mystery were we?

CHAPTER 10

"Jolene just loves these walks. She's going to miss all this dirt when we get back to the city." Lucy's voice was muffled as she positioned her camera in front of her and took shots of the woods as we walked.

"I'm sure she'll get used to it again, and it's not like she doesn't go to Central Park and Prospect Park. She's not exactly living in a concrete jungle."

"Thank God that we have that green space."

Lucy was clicking away furiously as we walked, and I was just enjoying the beauty of the late afternoon sky and weather. I studied the tree branches as we walked to see if I could see any birds or animals, but all I'd seen so far was what appeared to be a few lizards slithering away.

"Shall we go this way today?" I asked as we came to a fork in the woods. The path we'd gone on before looked clearer, but I was in an adventurous mood and wanted to take the road less traveled.

"Sure, lead the way." Lucy followed behind me as we stepped over a fallen tree trunk, Jolene jumping and running ahead as we changed direction.

"You never heard back from Gordon, right?" Lucy asked as we made our way through the forest.

"Not a thing, but I think he knows I'm suspicious and annoyed with him. I might not hear back from him for a while."

"That's too bad. I'd really hoped he was going to turn out to be a good guy friend for you."

"Yeah, me too. That first night we met in the village, he was so supportive and nice. I thought that we were at the beginning of a beautiful friendship. Now all I can think is that he was using me."

"Well, don't judge him before you know the truth, Savannah. It might not be as bad as we think."

"Yeah right." I was about to say something else when I noticed footprints in the dirt to the side of where we were walking. "Do those look like footprints or animal prints to you?" I walked over to check them out a little bit closer.

"Footprints," Lucy said as she came up behind me to survey the marks as well. "Definitely footprints. Looks like three different kinds, actually. See? The patterns all have different shapes."

"Hmm, yeah, weird." I walked back to the main path. "I wonder how recent they are."

"And who the three people were," Lucy added.

"And why they were at the side and not on the main path."

"It just keeps getting curiouser and curiouser," Lucy murmured. "Hey, have you written any poetry recently?"

"Actually, I wrote something this morning after I came out of the shower," I admitted. "Though I don't think it's any good."

"I wrote one this morning as well," Lucy replied. "How strange is that? Want to do a share as we walk?"

"Sure," I said. "Do you want to go first?"

"You go first."

"Okay." I walked for a few more seconds and then let the words spill from my mouth as if I were on stage. "Secrets, things you never told me, things I never should have known. Like your body, a muscular vision on a throne. You touched me, and in that instant I was yours. You touched me and pushed me down on all fours. You've got a secret, and it's something I shouldn't know. You've got a secret, and all I can think of is my glow. The way you touched me. The way your lips made me yours. You've got a secret, and I just want to close the door." I pretended to slam a door shut and then turned to Lucy, who was looking at me with understanding in her eyes.

"You love him." It wasn't a question, but a statement. "This isn't just a crush or an 'I'm falling for him' thing. You've already fallen." She spoke softly as if she didn't want to upset me or our surroundings by raising her voice.

"What did you think of the poem?"

"It was so beautiful. So raw." She looked me in the eyes. "It is a beautiful thing to know love, Savannah. I only hope he is worthy."

"Me too, girl. Me too."

"Okay, well, my poem is nowhere as near as heartfelt as yours, but here goes. I had a friend. I had a sister. I had a vision that spun like a twister. I was alone and living free. I was alone, but I didn't want to be. I had a vision of my own true love. With a smile so bright, and the angel spirit of a dove. I wanted it to be, so I waited all night. I wanted it to be, but my joy is floating like a kite. Up and away, out of my reach. I'll be forever alone. With not even my friend to teach."

"Oh, Lucy." I stopped and looked at her. "I didn't know you were so lonely."

"I'm not. Well, at least not all the time. It just hits me,

you know? In the middle of the night when I'm lying there, when the dreams won't take me away, and my brain just thinks."

"And you think about how it's just you?"

"Yeah. You know what I mean?"

"I know." I reached for her hand. "I totally get it."

"I thought I was just being a baby." She gave a rueful laugh. "It's not like it's every night, and you won't be gone forever."

"Did you ever feel that way when I was still there? In the apartment?"

"A little bit." She made a face. "I didn't feel alone because I always had you. And I love our friendship. But I did feel a little bit solitary and sad. Like I wanted more. Not that you weren't enough. But I wanted love. Or I should say, *want*. I want love too." She let out a deep sigh. "Sometimes I wonder if there's something wrong with me."

"You know you're gorgeous, right, Lucy?" I stared at my beautiful friend. "But I get it. I've felt the same way. I think it's something we all go through when we're single and don't necessarily want to be. You will find love as well, Lucy. And trust me, it's not all that. You could end up in a situation like me."

"I want love and an adventure as well, though. My life is so bor—oh, shit!" She stopped in her tracks and pointed ahead. "Shit, is that *blood*?"

"Say what now? Blood?" I looked over to where she was pointing and my eyes widened, "Oh my God, what is that?" We both ran over to the spot where, sure enough, liquid red had splashed the leaves on the ground. We looked at each other.

"Let's follow the trail," Lucy whispered.

I whistled to Jolene and together, the three of us followed the trickling spots of blood through the forest. We walked for about fifteen minutes, and then we spotted a small cabin nestled between the trees ahead.

"Shall we go in?" Lucy forged ahead without waiting for my answer. Jolene and I followed behind her.

"Please God, don't let us die today," I whispered under my breath as we reached the cabin door. Lucy opened the door slowly and we both grimaced as it creaked loudly. If there was anyone in there, they'd definitely know we were here.

Lucy walked in first and I followed. The cabin was small and appeared to be empty, but there was a rotting smell that hit me right in the stomach and made me gag. To the right of the room was a small wooden table with what appeared to be a ladies' blouse on top.

Directly to the back, there was a sink and a small window. Flies were buzzing around the sink and I walked over to it slowly. I stopped in front of the sink and what I saw made all the blood rush from my face.

I shrieked as I looked down at a thick slab of flesh and blood, just sitting there. "We need to leave, Lucy!"

Lucy took one look at my face and bolted for the door, but before I could follow her, an arm wrapped around my waist from behind.

I caught a glimpse of a rifle. Terror choked me so badly that I couldn't even scream, then darkness rushed up to claim my consciousness.

CHAPTER 11

"Savannah, are you all right?"

As I blinked back to consciousness, I was still too overcome with fear to realize what was going on. All I knew was that strong arms were locked around me, and I began to struggle. Finding my voice again, I started screaming at the top of my lungs.

"Savannah, stop screaming!"

Wade's commanding voice brought me back to my senses and I realized I was in his arms. He'd caught me as I'd fainted and was holding me tightly against him. His voice was firm, but he looked wild. His facial hair had grown out and his hair was unkempt and scruffy. I pushed him away.

"What the hell is going on here?" My heart gradually began to slow down, and I gulped a few deep breaths. "I thought you were away."

"Savannah, are you okay?" Lucy ran back into the cabin, her face white. She stopped as she looked between me and Wade and her eyes narrowed. "Who are you? What are you doing to my friend?"

"Who are you?" Wade turned back to me with a cocky smile. "Missed me so much you couldn't be by yourself?"

"No." I pushed him away and stepped back. "Lucy, this is Wade, my boss who's supposed to be on a business trip. Wade, this is Lucy, my best friend."

"Ah, the famous Lucy." Wade's voice was dry.

Lucy's eyes darted between us. "I feel like you guys have some things to discuss. I should take Jolene back to the house."

"Jolene?" Wade frowned. "How many friends do you have over right now?"

"Jolene is my baby."

"Your what?" His eyes narrowed and then it dawned on him. "Oh no, your mutt is here as well?"

"She's not a mutt." I poked him in the chest.

"I thought I told you no guests and your dog wasn't allowed?"

"Did you?" I peered at him with innocent eyes. How was he so sexy, even covered in dirt with specks of blood? I blinked as I remembered the flesh in the sink and the blood. "I think you owe me some explanations." I crossed my arms and looked at him. "What's going on here? Why are you here? What's with the blood? And that ... *stuff* in the sink?"

"I said I had to go away, I never said I was going out of town. That's an assumption you made, so that's on you."

"But ..."

"But what?"

Lucy spoke up again. "Don't let him double talk you, Savannah."

A wave of guilt washed through me because I'd forgotten she was still standing there. It was as if Wade had bewitched me, simply by being present.

I turned back to look at her again. "Now you see why I call him the worst boss ever, right?"

Lucy grinned and Wade let out a low hiss. I laughed and turned to look at him. "Or did you think you're the best boss ever?"

"I'm the best …" He paused as he looked behind me at Lucy. "I won't continue that comment as I don't want your friend to think poorly of you."

"Think poorly of me?" I raised an eyebrow.

"For sleeping with your boss." He winked at me. "That's one way to try and get ahead."

"You pig. It was nothing like that!" I gasped. "I never slept with you to get ahead. And what would I be getting ahead with? Being a personal assistant to another asshole?"

"And that's my cue to leave." Lucy stepped back.

"Wait, I'm coming with you." I moved away from Wade. "I'm sorry I disturbed you on your urgent business trip. The one that required you to leave first thing in the morning before I even woke up. Email me whatever tasks you need me to do and I'll do them."

"The meat in the sink is deer!" Wade shouted behind me as I stepped through the cabin door.

"What?" I turned to look back at him. "What are you talking about?"

"The meat in the sink." He walked to the cabin door. "It's venison. And the blood, it's from a deer and an elk."

"What are you talking about?"

"I was *hunting*, Savannah." He frowned. "What did you think it was?"

"I don't know. All I saw was blood all over the place and flesh in the sink. I thought …" My voice trailed off now. I didn't want to sound like a drama queen, but I had thought it was human flesh. I thought maybe some sort of Hannibal Lector-type psychopath was living in the forests behind his house, but I didn't want to tell him that. "Where's Henry?"

"He went with ... he went fishing." Wade frowned. "Why?"

'No reason." Now it was my turn to frown. "Why did you hide when we entered? And why did you have a rifle?"

"I didn't know who was entering my house, and I was protecting myself."

"But this cabin is on your property." I glanced at Lucy who was watching us and listening intently. "Why would you be hiding out like a fugitive?"

"I wasn't hiding out like a fugitive. I do this every month. I like to hunt. I like to live in nature. I like to be one with the land."

"Why did you leave before I woke up?"

He sighed. "Things are ... how can I put this? They're complicated."

"What's complicated? Why are you hiding out in the woods? Is it because we slept together?"

"Why would I hide in the woods because we slept together?"

"I don't know why you do half the things you do. Why are you such a creep?"

"How am I a creep?"

"You came into the house, didn't you? After you said you were going away. You left the French doors open and you left mud on the floor."

Instantly, his expression changed from exasperated to serious. "What are you talking about Savannah? What mud on the floor? And what doors? I haven't been back to the house since I left. I knew if I saw you, I wouldn't want to stay away."

"But then if it wasn't you ..." I shivered. So, it had been Gordon then?"

"Has anyone else been at the house?" Wade questioned me. "Asides from your mutt and friend?"

"No …" I sighed. "Well, Gordon. But …"

'The guy you met in town?" Wade sounded jealous. "What was he doing at my house?"

"He just wanted to keep me company, that's all."

"Where did he keep you company?"

"In your bed," I snapped. "Where do you think?"

"Do you think that's funny, Savannah?" Wade's face was dark. "You jump from my bed to another man's?"

"It's not like that. I was joking And stop twisting this on me. You're the one who lied."

"I didn't lie."

"Hey, guys, can we do this back at the house?" Lucy interrupted us. "I hate to get into the middle of this, but I don't feel comfortable leaving Savannah out here in the woods with you, and right now I don't think I feel comfortable being in the house by myself. Jolene's a lover, not a fighter."

"I'm coming, Lucy. I'm over this crap." I glared at Wade and shook my head. "This isn't even worth it. I'm done."

Wade glared at me. "What do you mean, you're done?"

"I mean, finite. I'm out. Deuces, baby."

Wade's expression grew dark. "We have a contract. You're not going anywhere."

"Keep your money. I'll keep my self-respect."

I turned toward the door, hoping I'd be able to hold the tears back until I was out of Wade's sight. I'd been through so much in the last two days, and he'd been here in the woods the whole time? Had he just left because he didn't want to be around me? Maybe he'd been hoping I would leave before he came back. Maybe this was all just a big joke to him.

"You signed a contract, you're not leaving." He grabbed my arm, turning me to look at him. "Please, Savannah." His voice cracked slightly.

I took a good look at him. There was something primitive and virile about him. He was a man of the woods. Or rather, a man who was one with the woods. He looked wild and primal, and even though I was still terribly angry with him, part of me was imagining what it would be like if he were to pick me up and carry me out into the woods and have his wicked way with me.

What the hell was my problem?

"Savannah, say you'll stay, please?"

I crossed my arms over my chest. "I want some answers, Wade."

"I will give you answers." He ran a hand through his unkempt hair. "Look, you and Lucy go back to the house with the mutt. I'll be up there in a couple of hours."

"You're not coming with us now?"

"No, I need to let Henry know I'm going back." His lips thinned. "He needs to take care of some stuff for me."

"What stuff?"

"Where did you find the mud? By the door or in the house?"

"What do you mean?"

"The person who came into the house, did they get all the way in?"

"I think they were in multiple rooms." I shivered slightly. "I felt like I was being watched. Wade, if it wasn't you, who was it?"

"I don't know." He looked uncomfortable for a few seconds and his eyes left mine. I wasn't a detective, but I certainly knew when someone was lying to me.

"Okay, well, I'm going now." I looked over at Lucy and nodded. "Shall we head back to the house?"

"Sure." She nodded back to me. She seemed to know not to say anything else.

"Will you still be there when I come in a couple of hours?" Wade sounded uncharacteristically hesitant.

"Maybe." I shrugged and walked away.

There were so many things I wanted to say to him, things I needed to get off of my chest, but my head and my heart felt heavy. I wasn't sure I even wanted to hear what he had to say anymore.

I was close to a breakdown. It had all been too much in the last few weeks, too much stress and worry. To be fair, the stress had started before I'd even gotten here, but my money stress had been different. It hadn't been all-consuming, not like this situation with Wade.

How could he have been on the property the whole time? I felt like a piece of me had been ripped out and I had no way of getting it back in.

Maybe I just needed to leave.

CHAPTER 12

"So … we're leaving now, right?" Lucy broke our stretch of quiet after a few minutes. She was surprisingly calm and gentle in her questioning and I knew that she knew that I was in a delicate state of mind right now. "Or not?"

"I don't know what to do." I chewed on my lower lip, contemplating my choices. "What do you think I should do?"

"I don't know." She shook her head. "He's cute." She half-smiled. "Even hotter than you described. I can see why you fell for him."

"He's not all that," I lied.

She laughed. "He's all that and a bag of chips. And he really seems to like you as well. His hands were all over you."

"Probably because he was debating whether or not to kill me."

"I think he was debating whether or not he wanted to just take you then and there." She looked at me sideways. "There was some serious heat in the air, didn't you feel it?"

"Well, after all that flesh and blood, how could I not?"

"Don't lie, you wanted him."

I blushed because I wondered if it had been that obvious to him as well. "I did. He's just so ... *masculine*."

"He's definitely a man's man. Nothing metrosexual about him," she agreed.

"Do you think he was lying? Do you think he was the guy that was spying on me?" I swallowed hard thinking about him watching me. "That would be so creepy."

"I don't think it was him. He sounded so shocked, almost angry." She shook her head. "I really don't think it was him."

"Do you think he knows who it was?" I sighed. "He knew *something*."

"He did know something." Lucy nodded in agreement. "Maybe it was his brother. What was his name again? Henry?"

"Yeah. Maybe."

But Henry was cool and fun and confident. It was hard to imagine him sneaking in and out of the house. I just didn't think it was Henry.

Lucy interrupted my thoughts. "So, are you going to press him for more information when he gets back to the house?"

"You bet I am. Also, why couldn't he just have left Henry a note? He left me a note when he left. He can't do the same with Henry?"

"Maybe he's worried Henry won't see the note. That cabin was a mess."

"That's putting it kindly." I managed a reluctant chuckle. "It looked like a hot mess."

"Do you know what I was wondering?" Her expression changed as she approached the house.

"What's that?"

"Where were the skins?"

"What skins?" I wrinkled my nose in distaste.

"The skins of the animals. He said they were hunting,

right? So, they killed at least one deer and one elk that we know of. You saw the meat in the sink, but where did they put the skins?" She whistled to Jolene to come inside with us as I opened the French doors. "I didn't see any hair, anyway, which we should have. We saw the blood, we saw the meat." She shrugged. "Just something I was wondering."

"Yeah, I have no idea." I shook my head. "Do people that hunt normally destroy the hides?"

"Depends." She shrugged. "I mean, let's be real, I don't really know the answer to that question. I think hunting is horrific."

"Me too." I nodded. "But I suppose it's good that he's not just hunting for sport. He's hunting and eating the meat."

"Is that really good, though? Does he need meat?"

"Well, we're not exactly vegetarians, Lucy. We can't be hypocrites."

"I'm not being a hypocrite. I just have problems killing innocent animals."

"All animals are innocent."

"You know what I mean." She frowned and headed to the fridge. "I'm getting some water, do you want some?"

"Yes, please." I nodded. "I'll get Jolene some water and food as well. She must be so thirsty and hungry."

"She's always thirsty and hungry." Lucy laughed. "I swear that dog could eat a horse and still end up begging for more when she was done."

"You know that's true. Come on, Jolene, it's dinner time."

Jolene came running into the kitchen, wagging her tail with excitement. I supposed that was one good thing, at least. She was having fun on her first adventure out of Manhattan.

"Here you go." Lucy handed me a glass of water. "I'm

going to go and shower now, but we can reconvene in thirty minutes? I've a feeling we're not leaving tonight, are we?"

"No, we're not leaving tonight." I gratefully sipped the water down and let out a small yawn. "I'm going to talk to Wade when he gets back. I want some answers, and I want them now."

"That's what I like to hear." Lucy smiled. "You demand the truth. And if he doesn't want to give it to you, we leave."

"Assuming he lets us," I said under my breath.

She frowned "I hope that's a joke, right? Because if that's not a joke, then we're leaving now."

"It's a joke."

I let out a hollow laugh. It was a joke, but if I was honest with myself, anything was possible. I didn't really know Wade Hart. As much as I wanted to believe that I did, what I knew didn't even scratch the surface.

CHAPTER 13

Jolene was curled up at the bottom of Wade's bed, snoring her little heart out. I smiled warmly as I watched her. It was nice watching my dog sleep in this room. But even though watching her filled me with happiness, I couldn't stop the worry from seeping into my bloodstream. My mind was constantly going over everything that had happened over the last couple of days, and I just couldn't figure out what was going on.

"I can't believe you're letting that mutt sleep on my bed." Wade walked into his room, his hair still wild and crazy, his eyes intent on my face. "You've been sleeping in here?"

"You didn't know that?"

"Would I be asking if I did?" He raised an eyebrow at me. "Miss me, did you?"

"No, but I put Lucy in my room. I didn't want to put her in another room without your permission."

"Shouldn't you have gotten my permission for her to stay in the first place?"

"I didn't know I had to get your permission for every little thing that I did."

"Well, seeing as I told you she couldn't be here in the first place, it might have been nice."

"Are you saying we have to leave?" I stood up.

"I'll snuggle next to Jolene myself if it means you'll stay." He walked over to the bed. I held back a laugh as he patted Jolene awkwardly on the back. He obviously was not comfortable around dogs. Had he never had a pet before?

"So, you're telling me that if I stay, you will sleep with Jolene?"

"Well, I don't really want to sleep with Jolene, but if that's the only way to get you to stay, then sure, I'll love her and kiss her and do whatever you want me to."

"Really?" I laughed.

"Really. I'll do whatever I want. You have the power." He paused and then smirked. "Well, when I say *whatever* you want, there are some limitations."

"What limitations?"

"I guess I'll just have to find out."

"Wow, you must really want me to stay."

"Isn't that obvious?"

"Why do you want me to stay?"

"I think you know the answer to that."

But of course, I didn't know. I studied his handsome face, wondering what he was thinking. Did he want me to stay because he wanted me in his bed—or was it more than that? What was in his heart? What was in his mind? Was he falling for me like I was falling for him?

I didn't know exactly what to believe. My mind was telling me that he liked me as more than just a one-night stand and as more than just one of his employees that he found attractive. My mind was telling me that this was something special, but I couldn't ignore the fact that he was keeping secrets, maybe a lot of them. I needed to know what he'd been talking about that night I needed to know how I could destroy him and Henry.

"What are you thinking about, Savannah?" Wade stroked my shoulder then cupped my chin and tilted my face up to him.

I stared up into his eyes, green and mesmerizing. They made me think of emeralds sparkling in the sunlight.

We stared at each other for what seemed like hours, even though I knew it was only a few minutes. There was an unspoken understanding between us, a buzzing, a chemistry, a feeling that I couldn't quite explain. It was like he was reading my thoughts and I was reading his, yet both of us were thinking in foreign languages that the other one didn't understand.

"I need to kiss you," he whispered. He leaned forward and pressed his lips against mine and it felt as if a million firecrackers were going off at the same time. The explosion in my heart was something I'd never felt before, but as his lips pressed against mine, the familiar feeling of his tongue warmed me. I melted against him.

Just one more time …

His fingers found my hair and he pulled just that little bit too hard so that my scalp tingled. The slight pain mixed with the ecstasy of his lips against mine made the kiss even more exciting and special. Even though I was standing on the ground, I felt like I was floating in the air. Wade made me forget everything except him.

"I want you, Savannah. I want you so badly. I want to taste you. I want to kiss you. I want to fuck you all night long."

"Wow, tell me what you really want," I teased as I pulled away from him. "Wade, we need to talk."

"Can't it wait?" His hand slid up to my breast. "I'm not sure I can focus on talking right now."

"So, you want to fuck me while you're still all dirty and full of mud and blood?" I wrinkled my nose. "Have you even had a shower yet?"

"Oops, I forgot I was dirty." He chuckled and pulled his shirt off.

I swallowed hard at the sight of his bare chest. Man, he was hot. How was a girl supposed to concentrate and keep her cool when presented with a specimen like this?

"Too dirty for you to do the dirty with me?" He grinned.

"You're assuming that I'm going to sleep with you at all."

"I think you want me as well." His fingers brushed against my hardening nipple.

I frowned and tried to get the conversation back on track. "What are you doing back already? I thought you were going to be hours. I've barely been back twenty minutes, and I told Lucy I'd hang out with her."

"Well, text her and tell her to wait."

"You didn't answer my question. How come you're back already?"

"I didn't want you to leave." He tugged on my shirt and I raised my hands so he could pull it off. "I didn't want you to be stubborn and try and teach me a lesson just because I wanted to go hunting."

I gasped as his fingers pulled the front of my bra down and my breast escaped from its cover. "It's not about you going hunting. It's about you—" I moaned as his lips fell to my nipple and he sucked. "Wade ..." I moaned. "We can't do this right now. I have to meet up with Lucy." I tugged on his unkempt hair, which caused him to suckle on my nipple even harder. Intense pleasure coursing through me. "Wade ..."

His hand moved between my legs and he rubbed me lightly. "Tell me you don't want me."

"I don't!" I ground out.

"Okay, then." He stepped back and let me go completely. "Do you want to shower first or should I?"

"Huh?" I felt slightly dazed.

"Or we could shower together." His fingers brushed against my trembling lips and then he grabbed my hand and brought my index finger to his mouth. He licked the tip of my finger and sucked on it lightly. Heat pooled between my legs. "But that's only if you want me to make you feel good."

"I don't need you to make myself feel good," I mumbled.

"Oh, yeah?" He pulled me towards him so that I could feel his very hard erection against my stomach. "Who else has been making you feel good?"

"I don't need any—"

"Was it Gordon?"

"No, it wasn't Gordon," I snapped, annoyed. "I can make myself feel good, by the way. I don't need you or any other man."

"I know you can make yourself feel good by yourself, but can you do it without images of me in your head?"

Images of our naked bodies pressed together suddenly filled my head. "Yes."

"Liar." He laughed as he kissed the side of my neck. "I bet when you last played with yourself you were thinking of me. I bet you were imagining my thick fingers on you, in you, touching you, wanting you. I bet you were thinking of my cock inside of you, making you come. I can feel you trembling right now just thinking about it."

"Do you only think about sex?"

"No, but when I'm with you, I can't help it." He unclasped my bra and let it fall to the ground. My breasts pressed against his chest while his warm hands ran up and down my back, massaging the knots of tension out of my muscles. I traced a line of dirt along his collarbone with my finger, marveling at how this new, primal side of Wade only made him more attractive.

The door suddenly opened. "Savannah, did you call me? I heard—oh!" Lucy stopped short in the doorway, her eyes wide as she took in the scene in front of her.

Heat rushed to my face and I instinctively crossed my arms over my bare chest. At least Wade and I weren't completely naked.

"I can come back." Lucy gave me a knowing smile. "Or rather, I can go into the kitchen and cook something and hang out until you're ready."

"That sounds like a good plan," Wade answered her, a wicked light in his eyes as he looked down at me. "And take the mutt with you. I don't know if Savannah wants her innocent little baby witnessing what we're about to do."

"Wade!" I glared at him, sure that my face was deep red now.

He laughed. "What?"

Lucy whistled and Jolene jumped off the bed to follow her out of the room.

"Was I lying or was I lying?" Wade asked as Lucy quietly shut the door behind her.

"That just seems so inappropriate!" I glared at him.

"As inappropriate as this?" He fell to his knees and reached up to pull my leggings and panties down.

He was now face to face with my pussy. I bit my lip. "Wade …"

"I'm hungry," he whispered, then he stood up and lifted me onto the bed where he pulled my clothes off completely. I was now naked except for a pair of wooly socks.

"Savannah, you smell good enough to eat," Wade growled as he nudged my legs open. I leaned my head back on the pillow and closed my eyes. Who was I kidding? I wanted this as badly as he did and I was too weak with lust to deny it. I cried out as his tongue licked the tip of my clit. The dart of pleasure coursing through my system was so intense that my entire body shook as if we were in an earthquake.

"You taste like home," he whispered as he took my throbbing bud into his mouth and sucked. I gripped the sheets and I tried to muffle my cries as he licked and teased me. When his tongue entered me, I could no longer hold back.

"Oh yes, Wade, don't stop!" I screamed, pushing his head into me. The feeling was so great, so amazing, that I had no shame. He must have liked how wild I was being because his tongue started moving faster. I could feel that I was close to an orgasm. He just needed to keep going. I was so close, *so* close. And then he pulled his tongue out and kissed back up my belly to my face.

"Why did you stop?" I moaned as he looked into my eyes with a teasing grin. "I was so close."

"You didn't deserve to come yet."

"Excuse me? What does that mean?"

"It means I didn't want you to come just yet."

"Oh, yeah?" I reached my hand down to my clit and rubbed myself. I closed my eyes and rocked back and forth, but Wade grabbed my hands and pulled them above my head.

"I think not, Savannah." He laughed and jumped off of his bed. He then opened the drawer I'd seen earlier with the sex toys and pulled out a pair of handcuffs.

"What are you doing?" I gasped as he clipped one end around one of my wrists.

"I can't trust you. You're being a naughty girl. Naughty girls get punished."

"What the …?" I groaned as he handcuffed my wrists together. "Wade, come on!"

"What?" He laughed as he kissed my left breast. "Don't worry, you'll come, just not quite yet."

"Wade!" I gritted my teeth and watched as he pulled his pants off. Even all dirty and sweaty, he was beautiful. "I want to touch you."

"You want to touch me or touch yourself?" he whispered against my ear as his cock twitched next to my thigh.

"I want to touch *you*," I whined as he kissed down the side of my neck, his fingers trailing over my breasts and to my belly. "*Please*."

"I'm going to fuck you slowly, Savannah. I'm going to need a lot more than a lightly whispered *please*." He licked the inside of my belly button. "I'm going to need you screaming out my name, begging me to make you come." He moved on top of me, kissing my lips again as he stared into my eyes. "And then I'm going to let you come." He groaned as the tip of his cock rubbed up against my wetness. "You're so turned on, aren't you? You want me so badly."

I closed my eyes. "No."

"Liar." He laughed as he rolled off of me and got off of the bed.

My eyes flew open. "Where are you going?"

"Rubbers." He laughed. "Don't worry, sweetheart. I'm going to let you come soon. Next time you get greedy, you might have to wait a little longer."

"What does that mean?"

He ripped open a condom wrapper and slipped it onto his hardness. "It means that I have a lot of things to teach you."

"Oh, yeah?"

"Yeah." He crawled onto the bed and ran the palm of his hands across my nipples. "Like who owns this body." His fingers slipped in between my legs again and rubbed.

I rolled my eyes at him. "*I* own my body, asshole, and if you think otherwise, you're in for a huge letdown."

I might want him more than I'd wanted anything else in my life, but I wasn't going to let him think he could just dominate me that completely. He could pleasure me, but he was never going to own me.

"Okay, you own your body." There was a light of respect in his eyes. "I forgot you're a modern girl."

"What does that mean?"

"I just meant that you are more sensitive to terminology."

"Uhm, what?" My voice rose and I started to feel heated. "What are you trying to say?"

"Let me take a step back." He grimaced. "That came out wrong. Your body is your own, and I'm happy—whenever you allow me—to pleasure you with mine."

"Uh huh, likely story."

"Have I totally ruined the mood?" He kissed me lightly on the lips and I did my best not to kiss him back. "Savannah, what if I promise to make you come harder than you've ever come before?"

"Are you going to take my handcuffs off?"

"Do you want me to take your handcuffs off?" He reached up and grabbed my wrists. "I'll do whatever you're comfortable with. I didn't mean to push anything on you. I forgot you're inexperienced."

"I don't need you to take them off," I grumbled because the truth was that there was something sexy about him being in control. "I just don't want you to think that you can do whatever you want with me."

"You don't think I can do whatever I want with you?" He laughed as he surveyed my face. "Not only can I do whatever I want with you, Savannah, I can also have you begging for it."

"You're so full of yourself." I tried to sound aloof but I

trembled as his fingers ran over my skin. I wanted to tell him to just leave me alone, but I knew my body would hate me if I did that. I wanted him too badly. As it was, I was barely able to concentrate on what we were saying. All I wanted was to feel him on top of me ... inside of me.

"Tell me what you want, Savannah, and you can have it."

"I want you, Wade. I need you." I moaned the admission and his eyes blazed with desire. Suddenly his lips and hands were everywhere, touching everything, kissing every sensitive spot, and making me want to crumble.

"Girl, have you missed my good loving?" He chuckled.

"Shut up, Wade," I whispered then his lips crashed down on mine. He entered me, and my entire body shifted against his in ecstasy.

He moved slowly at first, as if trying not to hurt me. But I tightened my legs and bit down on his lip to get him to move faster and he seemed to understand. He thrust into me faster and harder, and I cried out as my orgasm built up with an intensity I'd never imagined was possible. It was as if he'd taken me to the top of a mountain to hang glide and we were getting ready to jump. I needed to jump. I needed to feel the wind beneath my wings. I needed to fly. If he denied me for one more second, I thought I might combust. I needed him to take me home. I needed him to make me fly.

Wade seemed to know he couldn't tease me any longer. He moved inside of me as if he were putting pieces into a puzzle. The tip of his cock hit the right spot every single time and when his fingers reached down to gently rub my clit at the same time, that was all I needed to finally explode.

"Don't stop!" I gasped, writhing underneath him. He increased his pace and I felt my body shuddering underneath him as he also came inside of me. He grunted as he fucked me hard for a few seconds and then collapsed on top of me. He reached up to take my handcuffs off and then held me to him for a few seconds, his cock still inside of me. Eventually, he pulled out of me and slipped the filled condom off before settling back next to me.

He kissed the side of my face and grinned. "I think I should shower now. I'm what you would call a dirty boy."

"Yes, you are." I stifled a yawn as I ran my fingers down his chest. "In more ways than one."

"Well, I could be a clean boy if you want me to be. I'd love you to make me a clean boy."

I raised an eyebrow at him. "Do you want me to make you go to church?"

"Go to church?"

"So you can become a priest. Then you would be really clean."

"Are you telling me you have a fantasy of being with a priest?" He winked at me as I rolled my eyes. "Well, I don't mind role play. I can be your forbidden priest one night, and you can be my naughty nurse another night."

"No, I do not have a fantasy of being with a priest." I rolled my eyes at him. "That's sick and maybe even blasphemous."

"Oh no, don't tell me. You're a naughty Catholic schoolgirl with the requisite guilt that goes along with that."

"Three things: I'm not naughty, I'm not Catholic, I'm not a schoolgirl, and I have no guilt about anything."

"Well, that was four things. But I'm glad to hear that you're not feeling guilty as I'd very much like to do you again after we shower."

"After *we* shower?" I raised my eyebrows at him and laughed. "That's assuming a lot, isn't it?"

"Not really." He tilted his face to the head and grinned. "I'm thinking that your duties for the evening are to clean me."

"My *duties for the evening*? What duties?"

"Did you forget that you work for me?" He raised a single eyebrow. "And did you forget that your contract states that you can be called upon to work both day and night?"

"My contract doesn't state that I'll be wiping your butt." I rolled my eyes. "No way in hell you can say that my work duties include bathing you."

"I'm eccentric, what can I say? You didn't think you were making hundreds of thousands of dollars to make coffee and swim in my pool, did you?"

"Are you frigging kidding me, right now?" I glared at him.

"Well, I want you in the shower one way or the other, and I quite fancy a massage as well." He laughed. "Oh yeah, this could turn out to be an even better night than I had planned."

"Are you frigging kidding me?" I pulled the sheet up over me. "I should pack my stuff and leave right now."

"Are you going to?" He tugged the sheet back down. "Are you saying you find it so distasteful to touch me that you'd rather quit?"

"You really think you're the boss of me, don't you?"

"Did you hear what you just said, Savannah?" He burst out laughing. "I am quite literally the boss of you, so yes, I do think that."

"Grr!" I jumped up off of the bed. "Come on, then. And don't be shocked if skin comes off when I scrub you down. I'm not known for being gentle."

"I wouldn't expect you to be gentle. I wouldn't expect it at all." He stared at my naked body and grinned. "In fact, I quite like the idea of you being rough."

"Hmm, you would." I shook my head so that my hair cascaded down my back and walked towards the bathroom. "Hurry up if you want me to wash you. I'm not going to allow this to take all night. I still have to talk to Lucy later."

J. S. COOPER

"Do you really think Lucy expects you to come out after a session of lovemaking?" He waggled his eyebrows at me. "But then again, maybe you want to boast about my prowess to her and how good I make you feel."

"You're just insufferable, Wade Hart." I rolled my eyes again, even though a part of me wanted to laugh. I'd never met a man as infuriating as Wade before, and while his arrogance annoyed me, I couldn't help being amused by him as well.

"I'm insufferable, but I'm the best lover you ever had."

"Well, that's because you're the only lover I've ever had." I walked into the bathroom and over to the tub and turned the hot water on. "Do you have any essential oils?"

"Any what?" He looked confused.

"You know, peppermint, eucalyptus, lemon balm …?"

"No idea what you're talking about, so no."

"What about Epsom salts?" I tried to ignore the fact that we were both naked and he was looking at me as if he were still hungry.

"I have salt in the kitchen."

"Not table salt." I took a deep breath. "What about bath bombs?"

"Bombs?" He frowned. "Has all my good loving caused you to lose your mind?"

"*Bath* bombs, they release salts and oils into the bath to make it more relaxing. Some of them also make it foamy, but I usually add bubble bath if I want bubbles. But you have a spa tub so maybe it's a good idea not to add any bubble bath if we're going to run the jets. We could have bubbles up to the ceiling." I giggled at the expression on his face. "You have no idea what I'm talking about, do you?"

"No." He reached his fingers into my hair and leaned forward and kissed me lightly on the lips. "I have absolutely no idea."

"Is there anything going on, Wade?" I whispered, taking advantage of this moment of closeness between us. "Is there anything I should know about? Anything you're worried about?"

He stared at me for a few seconds, barely blinking and then he just shook his head, his dazzling eyes going slightly vacant. "Nope, there's nothing you need to know, Savannah. Nothing at all."

CHAPTER 14

"You look like you're thinking about something real hard." Lucy joined me out by the pool about an hour later and sat on one of the recliners next to me. "You okay?"

"Do you think I'm a fool, Lucy?" I sighed as I lay back. "Actually, maybe don't answer that."

"Why would I think you're a fool?" Lucy frowned.

"Because we just found Wade hiding out in the damn forest, and as soon as he gets back to the house, I'm in his bed, with no answers, but a whole lot of loving."

"A whole lot of loving?" She grinned. "Good loving, I hope?"

"If it wasn't good, would I be in this position?"

"I'm guessing that's a no."

"It's a huge no. He's got me hypnotized."

Lucy laughed. "Dick-motized."

"Not funny."

"So, I'm taking it you got no new information or you got a lot of new information that's no good, and you don't know how to tell me."

"No information." I sighed. "But his brother Henry is coming tomorrow for dinner."

"Oh, yay, another Hart brother," Lucy said sarcastically. "Do you think we can get this one to talk?"

"Well, I was hoping-slash-thinking that you would be able to get him to talk, and I'd work on Wade."

"How the hell am I supposed to get him to talk?" Lucy pursed her lips. "I've never even met the guy."

"You could work your magic powers on him."

"What magic powers?"

"I don't know. Flirt." I laughed when she made a face. "I'm not trying to pimp you out. I'm just saying this could be a strategy to get more information."

"How do we even know that he knows something?"

"Because I heard Wade on the phone with him, remember? It's both of them I can ruin."

"I cannot believe you're trying to pimp me out to your boss's brother," Lucy grumbled. "I know I'm desperate, but I'm not *that* desperate." Then she paused. "But just so I know, is he as hot as Wade?"

"Some might say he's even hotter."

It was true. Not that I found Henry hotter. I was all into Wade, but I could see that people who preferred a smiling face to a dark angsty one would very much prefer Henry.

"So, what's the plan with Wade?" Lucy changed the subject and I sat up.

"What do you mean?"

"How do you feel about him now and do you trust him more than before? And did he tell you anything about why he was in the woods?"

"He keeps saying that he just wanted to go hunting." I shrugged. "I'm not a hunter, I don't know how that goes. And no, he's given me nothing else. And I don't know if I trust him any more than I did before."

"I can see why you've fallen for him. There's something about him." Lucy looked thoughtful. "He has a commanding presence."

"Yeah." I shivered as I thought about the way he'd handcuffed my wrists together. "He likes to be in charge."

"And from the looks of it, the sex is amazing."

"You can't even imagine. I didn't even know it could feel like this." I licked my lips. "It's crazy, but it feels like more than sex. It really does. It feels like we have a real connection."

"That's dangerous, Savannah." Lucy looked concerned. "I don't mind if you have sex with him still, that's your right, but please don't let your emotions get involved. Not any more than they already have. And if you think you can't control your feelings, then you need to stop the sex. Immediately."

"Why are you always right?"

"Because I was born that way." She laughed. "Do you want to go for a swim? I've never had a midnight swim before."

"Aren't you tired?" I laughed. "And you do know that it's not midnight, right?"

"I know it's not midnight, but I also know that tomorrow night I might not be here, so I want to enjoy it while I can."

"You think we might be gone tomorrow?"

"Savannah, I honestly don't know. Everything is happening so quickly and it's all so crazy. What if we find out that the meat in the sink wasn't a deer ..." She paused.

"What's that look for?"

"I'm just saying—remember he said it was deer and elk?"

"Yeah, so?"

"So, he killed a deer and an elk and we see no hair, no bones, no antlers and barely any meat."

"Oh." I swallowed hard as I processed her words. "So … then what was it?"

"I don't know."

"You think he's bad, don't you?"

"I don't know." She shook her head. "If I had a really bad feeling, we'd be out of here, and I certainly wouldn't have let you sleep with him again. But the more I think about everything, nothing is really adding up."

"I hate this," I grumbled. "I feel like we still know nothing."

"I think we know a whole lot more than we realize." She played with her fingers and sighed. "We just need to unlock that knowledge."

"Easier said than done."

"Yes, it is." She jumped up. "So, can we swim now? Tomorrow our minds will be fresh and we can think more."

"Sure." I stood up. "Let's go to your room and change and then come back out."

"Do you think that Wade will mind?"

"No." I shook my head. "I just gave him a massage and a body scrub. He's probably sleeping."

"A body scrub?" Lucy raised an eyebrow. "Should I even ask?"

"No." I blushed, remembering how I'd gone from rubbing him down with my hands to massaging him with my breasts. I'd never had a bath with a man before and I'd never had sex with a man in the bath before. It had been hot and sexy, but I wasn't quite ready to tell Lucy how I'd ridden my boss to orgasm as he'd squeezed my breasts and pinched my nipples.

Some things needed to remain behind closed doors.

CHAPTER 15

"Lucy, you really didn't have to help me make dinner. I could have done it by myself." I opened a packet of cheese. "But I'm not going to lie. I'm so grateful to you for helping. This is really going to be a delicious dinner. Wade is going to be shocked."

"I bet." Lucy laughed. "I guess he must actually like you a little bit because you're still employed and we both know that you can't cook for shit."

"Yes, I can," I objected. "I make the best cheese on toast made to man."

"Ha ha, but man cannot live on cheese alone."

"You wanna bet?" I grinned and then picked up the grater. "Do you want me to grate this entire block of cheese?"

"Yup, we're going to make potatoes au gratin." Lucy nodded. "You can either grate the cheese or scallop these potatoes."

"I don't even know what it means to scallop potatoes." I laughed. "I'll stick to grating the cheese."

"You took the steaks out of the freezer right? They're defrosting?"

"Yup." I nodded. "We can season them next."

"Awesome. I'll season them, and you can make the salad."

"I do make a mean salad."

"Sure." Lucy laughed. "So what time is Henry arriving?"

"He's going to be here at about 6 p.m. I think that's what Wade said."

"And Wade is still out, right?"

"Yeah." I nodded. "He's been out all day."

"How was last night when you went to bed?"

"He slept and I slept." I sighed. "He was pretending to be asleep when I went back to the room after our chat."

"How do you know he was pretending?"

"He was snoring loudly." I made a face. "And he never snores. He's such a bad actor."

"You didn't call him out on it?"

"Girl, if he wanted to pretend he was sleeping, let him pretend. I don't even care. I'm over him and his lies."

"Aww, man." Lucy rubbed me on the back, trying to comfort me. "Hopefully, tonight leads to some answers."

"Do you really think it will?"

"Mm ... no, but one can always hope."

"You really don't have to seduce Henry, by the way. I was just joking last night."

"I know you were joking, and honestly, it doesn't even matter if you weren't. There's no way in hell that I'd seduce someone just to get information."

"You say that now ..." I laughed and then yelped as I cut myself on the grater. "Ugh, this sucks. Did you say you also needed me to cut some yellow onions?"

"Yes, please." Lucy nodded at the onions and then started singing an old Rosemary Clooney song that she loved called "Mambo Italiano."

As I sang along with her, some of my anxiety started to dissipate, replaced with determination. I had no idea why

Wade wanted to have this dinner with Henry tonight. And I had no idea where he'd been all day. All I knew was that enough was enough. I needed answers. I was going to *demand* answers. Something was up and I wasn't going to let it go until I knew what was going on.

Lucy stopped singing. "Oh, yeah—have you heard from Gordon yet?"

I shook my head. "Still nothing."

"Hmm, very suspicious." Lucy put the sliced potatoes into a large bowl. "Well, hopefully,

we'll have some information soon. I have the request in with the library to get access to some newspaper articles I couldn't find online."

"What articles?" I looked up from the onions I was chopping. "You didn't tell me about any articles."

"I went online and used JSTOR and some other library searches. I found a slew of articles about Joseph Hart, Wade Hart, Henry Hart, and Louisa Hart. Many of them have been archived, but the great thing about the library is that they have microfiche. I'm having everything sent to me. I'll be able to go through the articles and find out more about these Hart men who've gotten entangled in our lives."

"*Our* lives?"

"Well, at first it was just your life, but now I'm invested, and I want to know what's going on."

"Yeah, me too. When will you get the articles? I can help you read through them."

"I'm not sure." She poured some heavy cream into the bowl and then salt and pepper. "Hopefully soon."

"Those are some weird ingredients." I raised an eyebrow. "Are you sure you know what you're doing?"

"Savannah, are you seriously questioning my culinary skills? You, who thinks putting Pillsbury cinnamon rolls into the oven makes you a baker?"

"That was only once and they turned out pretty good."

She just shook her head at me. I glanced at the clock on the wall and realized we only had an hour left to finish the meal and get changed. Where was Wade and when would he be back? I was just about to text him when I heard him coming through the front door. He'd brought Henry with him and I could hear the two men talking as they made their way down the corridor towards the kitchen.

"Something smells good," Henry said as they entered the kitchen.

I wanted to answer him, but the look on Wade's face stopped me. He wasn't smiling and he wasn't angry, he was just there, staring, watching, studying me, and it made me feel like I was the only woman in the world that had ever existed. An idea for a poem sprang to mind and I wanted to rush out of the room and write it down, but I knew that I would look weird if I did that.

"I guess no one is going to introduce me." Henry stepped forward and offered his hand to Lucy. "I'm Henry, Wade's better-looking brother."

"I'm Lucy, Savannah's wiser and smarter best friend."

Henry chuckled. "Wiser and smarter, huh? I didn't know there was a difference."

"Are you asking me for the definitions or are you just trying to be difficult?" Lucy shot back and I blinked at her in surprise. I'd never seen Lucy combative before, but as I saw the twinkle in her eye, I wondered if she were actually flirting.

"If you have the definitions to give me, sure go ahead." Henry ran his hands through his hair and leaned back as if he were highly enjoying the conversation he was having.

"No, thank you, Lucy." Wade cleared his throat and put his arm around his brother's shoulder. "Henry, stop teasing the poor girl. You don't want her to think that both of the Hart brothers are crazy."

"Crazy sexy?" Henry raised an eyebrow and then winked at Lucy. He was as big a tease as Wade.

"Is there such a thing as crazy sexy?" Lucy responded sassily. "You're either crazy *or* sexy, and I have a feeling you know which one you are."

"I do know, but do you?" Henry laughed "Okay, we should leave you both for now, but I'm excited for dinner and to catch up with you both again soon."

"Let's go, Henry." Wade kissed me on the lips. "I'll be talking to you later, Ms. Savannah Carter." He winked and smacked me on the bottom and then both brothers left the kitchen. I looked over at Lucy who was silently laughing.

I glared at her. "This isn't funny!"

"I know," she said, suddenly looking serious. "I think we're both in a whole heap of trouble, and all I can hope is that we get some answers soon."

CHAPTER 16

"They say the way to a man's heart is through his stomach, and I feel like you two really want to win our hearts." Henry grinned up at Lucy as we finished setting all the plates on the table then looked down at his plate of steak, potatoes, and vegetables. "This looks delicious. I didn't realize how hungry I was."

"Give it a break, Henry." Wade sounded annoyed. He'd been moody since he'd gotten back home. We hadn't spoken all day, and I wasn't sure if he was deliberately avoiding me. It felt like he'd put a barrier up between us. Maybe he wished he was still in the forest hunting.

"Well, I hope you enjoy it, Wade." I took my seat next to him. "I know what a picky eater you are."

"Do you really think I'm a picky eater?" He looked at me with a smirk as his hand found my knee until the table and squeezed it gently.

"Yes, you're the pickiest."

"That's not what you said last night."

I felt my face flush. "Really, Wade?"

Henry laughed. "And he says *I'm* immature."

Wade's hand moved up my thigh and I slapped it off. "What do you think you're doing?"

"Nothing." He blinked innocently as he picked up his knife and fork. "Thanks for cooking, ladies. I have to agree with my brother, this looks amazing."

"Well, it's not like I had a choice," I pointed out. "This is my job."

"Touché." Henry laughed again. "Before we start, let me get us some drinks. Red wine for everyone? I think we have some nice bottles in the cellar."

"You have a wine cellar?" I looked over at Wade. "Why didn't I know about this?"

He smirked. "I didn't want you drinking me out of house and home. Good wine is expensive."

"You're such an asshole."

"Because I won't let my assistant drink my thousand-dollar bottles of wine?"

"I'm just your assistant now, huh?"

"Well, after hours, you're my bedroom whore." I smacked him hard in the arm. He laughed, though the laugh sounded hollow. "It was a joke, Savannah. You know it was a joke, right?"

"It was a tasteless joke," I snapped. "I'm so done with you."

"Savannah, I apologize, you're not my bedroom—" He stopped himself. "I'm not even going to say the word again."

"You know the truth is often said in jest, brother?" Henry's voice held a hint of amusement.

Wade turned a dark frown in Henry's direction. "I will make you leave if you keep this up."

"Well, I'll just keep my mouth shut and enjoy my food and the company of two pretty women." Henry cut into his steak and then paused. "Oops, I almost forgot I said I'd get the wine."

"Stay." Wade stood up. "I'll go and get some bottles."

"Would you like me to help?" I offered. "So I can see where the wine cellar is?"

"No," he growled. "It's in the basement, and I don't want you down there." He made for the door. "I'll be back in a moment."

"Okay." I picked up my fork, trying to act like I didn't care.

From across the table, Lucy caught my eye. *What's up with the basement?* she mouthed to me. I shrugged in response. *We need to explore later.*

Okay, I mouthed back.

Lucy smiled brightly at Henry. "So, Henry, Savannah tells me you don't live in the house here with Wade?"

"No way." He laughed. "That definitely wouldn't work out well. We're both too alpha for that."

"So, where do you live?"

"I travel quite frequently. Right now, I'm staying in another house on the property." He took a bite of potatoes and moaned appreciatively. "This is absolutely amazing, by the way."

"Thanks," Lucy said. "So, you're staying in the hunting cabin as well?"

"Hmm?" Henry looked up at her, a slight wariness on his face. "Yeah."

"Are you hunting bears too?" Lucy cut into her meat.

"Bears?" Henry laughed. "What bears? We have deer, elk, moose, squirrels, rabbits. I've never seen any bears. Did Wade say he was hunting bears?" He shook his head. "Next thing you know he'll be saying he caught Big Foot red-handed as well."

"Oh, maybe I misunderstood." Lucy laughed carelessly. "I thought there were bears up here. So, you're a big hunter as well?"

"Not really." He shook his head. "It was really my dad and Wade that were into the hunting. I was more into the eating." He took another bite of his meat. "In fact, maybe you girls could cook up some of the venison Wade shot? Maybe a nice stew. I love me a venison stew."

"Maybe." Lucy's smile stiffened, and I knew that it was never going to happen. "So, Henry, do you have any other brothers or sisters?"

"Wow, what is this, twenty questions?" Henry chuckled again, but he didn't sound quite so amused anymore. "I have one brother, Wade, and that's it."

"No other siblings? Half or step …?" Lucy's voice trailed off as Wade walked back into the room a bottle of red wine in each hand.

"Wade, Lucy was just asking if we have any other siblings." Henry looked up at his brother and made a face. "What do you think?"

"Our mother seems to think it's a possibility." Wade put the bottles down on the table. "Savannah, do you mind getting some wine glasses, please?"

"Sure."

I stood up and walked to the kitchen, my mind racing. Lucy was really going hard tonight, maybe too hard. What if she asked a question that the brothers didn't like? Henry was joking around and being goofy, but what did that really mean? Gordon had been all lighthearted and goofy as well when I met him, and I was pretty sure that had all been a front.

I reached for the wine glasses. Where the hell was Gordon? How could he have just disappeared and not even have sent me a message? At the end of the day, I'd thought we were friends.

Glasses in hand, I leaned back against the counter and took a few deep breaths. A wave of sadness passed through me. Maybe my anxiety about this whole ordeal was finally catching up with me.

Or maybe I was just disappointed in myself. Maybe I should have told Gordon I was on his side. Maybe I should have told him I knew his secret and that I wanted to help him find the answers. Instead, I'd been more loyal to Wade—and why? Just because I was attracted to him? Nothing I knew about Wade told me I could trust him more than Gordon.

Well, nothing on a conscious level. In my gut, I still felt there was something strange about Gordon's conduct and that it had nothing to do with Wade and me.

I was driving myself crazy. It all seemed to be one crazy riddle after another. And now Wade didn't want me to go into the basement—I didn't even know where the basement was! I'd been throughout the house and never even seen the door.

What secrets was he hiding down there?

"Did you get lost?" Wade entered the kitchen. "Or did you have to wash the glasses or something? What's taking so long?"

"Sorry, I just needed a minute to myself."

I didn't look into his eyes. I didn't want us to have that connection. I needed to start distancing myself from him. Lucy was right: the closer I got to him, the harder it was going to be to accept the possible truth and move on.

"You're not mad at me, are you?" He stepped close and held my chin, lifting it so that my eyes were gazing into his.

"Why would I be mad at you?" I blinked, trying not to let myself be hypnotized by those mesmerizing eyes. They seemed to be looking into my very soul.

"Because I called you my bedroom whore. I suppose I could have said wench, but I don't think you would have liked that either."

"Neither one of those comments are funny, Wade." I tried to sound stern, but my body trembled as he moved closer to me.

"I know, but I never said I was funny." He kissed the side of my cheek. "Did I tell you how hot you look tonight in that dress?" His fingers tweaked the hem. "How I just want to slide my hand all the way up and—"

"Let's take the glasses into the dining room. I'm sure Henry and Lucy must be wondering what's happening."

"They can wait," he whispered, kissing down my neck lightly, his hands now on my waist, pulling me into him. "I think we have time for a little fun, don't you?"

"No," I whispered as his hands lightly grazed my breasts. "Wade?"

"What?" His fingers brushed my hardening nipples. "Can I help it if I'm attracted to you? I want you so badly right now." He pushed his hardness against my belly.

I whimpered at the feel of him. "Wade, we're in the middle of dinner. This is not appropri—oh!" I gasped as his tongue slid into my mouth and then we were kissing passionately. His body was warm against mine and heat curled deep within me in response. I wanted him so badly, but there was no way I was going to let him have a quickie with me.

"Wade, no … we have to go back to the dining room." I pushed him away from me.

"I should spank you," he grumbled, but he stepped away and straightened his jacket. "So, what's with Lucy and all these questions?"

"What do you mean?"

"Why is she grilling me and my brother?" His tone was a little too casual. Maybe Lucy and I weren't the only ones trying to find something out.

"I have no idea what you're talking about, Wade." I lifted

the glasses. "Let's go back. I'm hungry, and the food is getting cold."

"You can't make excuses all night, Savannah." He smiled slyly. "You will succumb at some point."

"You wish, Wade Hart. You wish."

"I've got the first bottle open." Henry stood up as we walked back in. "Everyone ready for a generous pour?"

"I'm more than ready." Lucy's voice was chipper but she flashed me a concerned look.

I gave her what I hoped was a reassuring smile in response. It was the best I could do in that moment. I was close to crumbling.

"I'll have some as well, thanks." I sat back down and waited for Henry to hand me a glass. When he handed it to me, I took a small sip. "Wow, this is absolutely amazing. What is it?"

"This is a Pomerol Bordeaux." Henry smiled and took a sip. "Aw, yes, one of my favorites. This is a 2011 bottle from Petrus," he said as if I'd heard of the company.

"We should get a couple of bottles." Lucy grinned at me. "I wonder if they have them at Whole Foods or Trader Joes."

"They don't." Wade smirked. "A bottle will set you back about thirty-five hundred dollars."

Lucy blinked. "You mean ... thirty-*five* dollars?"

Wade laughed. "Three thousand five hundred dollars."

"Yeah, I guess we won't be buying any bottles," Lucy agreed.

"That's an expensive bottle of wine." I sipped it a little more slowly this time. "But now I understand the saying you get what you pay for."

"Well, this one pairs perfectly with the meal." Wade beamed as he sat back down. "Now let's enjoy our dinner."

"Yes, boss." I cut into my meat and continued eating.

Silence descended on the table. To anyone looking in from the outside, we probably would have looked like two happy couples enjoying a nice dinner together. But outside eyes couldn't feel the tension in the air that was building up with every second. I felt like I could cut it with a knife, and I almost jumped out of my skin when Lucy started talking again.

"So have you guys met Savannah's friend, Gordon?" she asked as she finished up the remains of the Caesar salad on her plate.

"No. I've heard about him a lot, though." Wade poured everyone some more wine. "Do you like him?"

"I haven't gotten to meet him yet," Lucy replied. "But Savannah tells me he looks a lot like you guys. And I was wondering if he might be an illegitimate brother."

"What?" Wade's eyes flew to mine and his eyes narrowed. "You never told me that!"

"Told you what?" I muttered, glaring at Lucy. What was she thinking?

"So, do you think that he could be your brother?" she prodded and then looked at Henry. "What do you think?"

"What do I think?" He held his wine glass in his hand and swirled the liquid around for a few seconds. "I think I'd have to ask my dad if he sired another child for me to know the answer, but seeing as our dad is dead, that will be kinda hard."

"That's enough, Henry." Wade jumped up, fury evident on his face, and then he turned to me and Lucy. "I don't know what you guys are playing at, but you both need to step back. Savannah, I told you that you can't have friends here or your mutt, and you disobeyed me. We're going to have to talk about this later."

"Oh, Wade," Lucy called out to him as he walked out of the room.

"What?" he snapped.

"Are you going to get rid of Savannah, just like you did with your last assistant?"

"What the hell is that supposed to mean?" His eyes narrowed.

"Why don't you tell us?" she said in a low voice.

"Henry!" Wade barked at his brother. "Let's go." And with that, he was gone. I looked at Lucy who was grinning, her eyes lit with excitement.

"You really went and poked the bear, didn't you?" Henry shook his head as he stood up and stared down at Lucy. "You're a very stupid girl."

"Am I really?" She glared up at him, looking even more beautiful than normal.

"Yes." He met her gaze. "And if I were a stupid man, I'd kiss you right now." He rubbed his lips and sighed as he straightened his back. "But, unfortunately for me, I'm not stupid." And with that he turned around and left the room as well.

I counted to five under my breath and then I exploded on Lucy. "What the hell are you doing? Are you trying to get us kicked out?"

"Would that be so bad? Wade is a psycho."

"He's not a psycho!"

"Girl, I hate to say it, but whatever he's hiding is huge." She bit down on her lower lip. "He went from flirting and happy to explosive in a matter of minutes. We're getting close, girl."

"Are we?"

"I think so."

"You keep saying that, but we still don't know anything."

"But that's where you're wrong, Savannah. You keep saying we know nothing, but that's not true. We actually know a lot. The problem is we don't know what we know."

"Huh? You're confusing me."

"Because we don't know everything, we don't know what the information actually means."

"So we don't know anything?"

Lucy took another sip of wine and looked thoughtful. "Do you think Henry was going to kiss me?" she mused. "Like if you weren't in the room, do you think he would have gone ahead with it? Or do you think he was just teasing me?"

"What the hell, Lucy?" I frowned. "We were just talking about this mystery, why are you talking about kissing Henry now?"

"There's something about him." She smiled dreamily. "I wouldn't mind him being my first."

"Oh, hell no." I groaned. "Girl, we're literally in the middle of getting kicked out of the house, and you're asking about Henry?"

"I know." Her cheeks turned pink. "I'm not sure what's come over me. I guess it's that Hart magic you've been talking about."

I sighed. "We can't both be mesmerized by the Hart boys … but it did look like you guys had a lot of chemistry," I admitted.

"He's gorgeous, though." Lucy shook her head. "He wouldn't really be flirting with me."

"Lucy, you do know that you're gorgeous as well, right?"

"Hold on." She put her fingers to her lips and stood up and walked slowly to the door. "Come," she whispered, motioning for me to join her. I stood up, took another long swig of wine, and walked over to join her. "Listen," she said as I stood next to her. I could hear the distant echo of shouting. "Someone is pissed at someone. Come on, let's get a little closer."

We tiptoed towards Wade's office and stopped in the hallway. My heart was pounding so loudly I wondered if Henry and Wade would hear it. If either of them opened the door and walked out, they would see us standing there and they would know that we were eavesdropping.

"You just don't know when to keep your big mouth shut, Henry!" Wade was shouting. "What the hell are you trying to do?"

"Obviously, I wasn't going to say anything …" The rest of Henry's sentence was muffled and we couldn't hear what he said.

"Do you want them to fucking find out? Do you want to go to jail?"

"We're not going to go to jail."

"We're fucking going to get locked up. What we did, it's criminal! Do you understand what that means? And it's all going to blow up in our faces."

"They have no idea, Wade. Trust me. They …" Muffled again.

"They are asking too many questions. What if they venture …" Now Wade was muffled. Lucy and I stood there, clutching each other's arms, eyes wide. I didn't even dare to breath. I was scared that even my heart beat was too loud.

"They're not going to venture …" Henry's voice was up and down. "They don't even know how to get there …"

"What if they find …"

"They won't."

Find what? I mouthed to Lucy.

She just shook her head. "Shh!"

I wanted to tell her that her shush was louder than the words I'd mouthed, but I kept my lips closed.

"Wade, at some point we're going to have to figure this out. We can't just keep—"

"Henry, enough. You need to stop flirting with Lucy and leave."

"She's cute, why can't I flirt with her? It's okay for you to be fucking Savannah on all fours, yet …" There was an inarticulate yell. "God damn, what was that for?"

"Don't talk about Savannah, like that!" Wade growled and we heard a loud bang. "She's not just some—"

"Wade, I don't think this is about me, this is about Savannah." Henry's voice had gone from outraged to amused. "She's the one that's causing all this trouble. Maybe it's not me that needs to leave."

"I don't know what the hell to do!" Wade's voice rose again. "She can't be here. Especially now she's questioning me and figuring things out. If she finds out …"

His voice became muffled again, and I inched closer to the door. Lucy tried to grab my arm to stop me, but I shook her off. I needed to hear more. I needed to hear everything. I needed to know what was going on. What was Wade so afraid of?

"And what's she going to do if she finds out?" Henry said quietly.

"That's the problem, I don't know." Wade sounded like his voice was going to crack. "But she's getting too close."

"Like the last girl."

"Yeah, and I don't want what happened to her to happen to Savannah."

"So what next?"

"I have to send her away for good." Wade sounded as distraught as I felt. "I have to protect her."

"From who?" Henry asked the words I myself wanted to ask.

"From me."

I heard footsteps and panicked. I stepped back, grabbed Lucy, and pulled her towards my bedroom. I closed the door behind us and locked it.

"What did you hear?" Lucy asked me, her face pale.

"Not much." I pulled her towards the bed and we sat down on the mattress. "I think Wade is going to send me away. He thinks we've been asking too many questions. And he's worried he'll have to do something to me to shut me up."

"Do what to you?"

"I don't know." I shook my head. "I just don't understand. It doesn't make sense. There's something in the basement they don't want us to find."

"Oh?"

"Henry said something about what if they venture, and Wade cut him off and said they—meaning us—won't find it."

"In the basement?"

"Well, he didn't say the basement, but what else could it be? He was pissed off that Henry mentioned it, remember? And he told me to stay away."

"True." She nodded. "So, what's in the basement?"

"Or rather who." I felt faint. "Lucy, what if the last assistant is dead?"

"What?" She sounded sick. "Like murdered?"

"Well, what if it wasn't a murder exactly?" I knew I was grasping at straws. "What if some accident happened or something, and she died and they hid the body in the basement?" I wrapped my arms around myself. "And they're worried I'll find the body and they'll go down for murder."

"Oh, shit," Lucy murmured. "But then why wouldn't they just say that it was an accident?"

"I don't know, maybe it was shady?" I took a deep breath and buried my head into my hands. I was close to tears and close to pulling my hair out. I'd never felt so frustrated in my life.

"Oh, Savannah," Lucy hugged me to her. "Are you okay? This is a lot, isn't it?"

"He wants me to leave." I shook my head as I felt tears starting to come. "Why does he want me to leave? I would understand."

"You'd understand if it was an accident, but what if it wasn't?" Lucy whispered the words I didn't want to hear. I looked up. There was a sadness in her eyes that made me cry even harder. "Maybe we should be happy that he's going to let you leave." She stroked my head. "It's better than him locking you up as his slave or something."

"Locking me up as his slave?" I smiled through a hiccup. "What?"

"Haven't you read any of those dark romance books? There's always some hot brooding guy that kidnaps some sweet woman and than has her as his sex slave."

"Lucy, what are you talking about?" I giggled as I wiped my tears away. "I wasn't kidnapped, and I don't think Wade wants me as his sex slave."

"I know, but I just wanted to see you smile." She tapped me on the nose. "You're strong girl. The Hart brothers might be hot, but we're strong and smart. And I promise you that no matter what happens, you're going to be okay."

"I just never felt this way before, you know?" I sighed. "I love him, and I just wish he could trust me and —"

"It's not about you, Savannah," Lucy whispered. "I wouldn't be surprised if he did have some sort of feelings for you. I've seen the way that he looks at you."

I snorted. "That's just lust."

She shook her head. "It's more than that. He stares at you when you're not even looking. He watches you. He studies you. And there's a light in his eyes. I can tell. He has feelings for you. He is fighting it, but it's more than lust. When you laugh or smile, he lights up. Not his face, but his eyes. I can see it in his eyes. You know I can read people well."

"Can you though?" I smiled a little through my tears. "So you've noticed him watching me?"

"I didn't want to say because feelings make it so much harder to walk away, but I won't have you thinking he doesn't care. But yes, there's a way he watches you walking and talking, and there's a softness that comes over him when he's talking to you and teasing you." She brushed a lock of hair out of my face. "If this wasn't such a crazy situation, I'd say it was sweet. He's protective of you."

"Maybe he's acting?"

"No, because he's not doing it obviously." She shook her head. "He's not that way to lull you into a sense of safety. In fact, I think he tries hard to make you hate him a little bit."

"Really?"

"Yeah." She nodded. "I can see that he pushes you away. He wants you to be mad at him."

"But why?"

She shrugged. "Why do guys ever do anything? I don't understand them. I don't think women ever understand men. My mom still doesn't understand why my dad does the things he does." She squeezed my hand. "Tomorrow we need to look for that basement, okay?"

"Okay." I nodded and smiled. "We're crazy, you know that, right?"

"I do." She laughed.

Knock knock!

Lucy and I jumped at the noise and looked at each other.

"Savannah, are you in there?" Wade's voice came through the door.

"Yes?" I called back.

"Can I talk to you?"

"Go ahead." I remained sitting on the bed.

"In person?"

"Anything you want to say to me can be said in front of Lucy."

"Savannah, can you open the door?"

"I can."

"Will you please stop being difficult?" He sounded annoyed.

"Or what? Are you going to command me to open the door?"

"Don't make me."

"Or what?"

"Savannah, open the damn door!"

"Are you going to leave him standing there?" Lucy grinned at me. "He's pissed."

"Good. I'm pissed off with him as well."

"Savannah?"

"I'm not ready to come out. Lucy and I are talking."

"You left the dishes on the table." He sounded stern. "You still need to tidy up."

"You do it!"

"What?" He sounded shocked. "Don't I pay you to do the dishes?"

"Yeah, I know I'm your maid, but tonight I'm off the clock, so deal with it yourself."

"Savannah, you're the worst employee I've ever had."

"Well, you're the worst boss."

"Savannah, open the door, now!" He banged on the door again. "Savannah!"

"Dude, chill. She doesn't wanna deal with you and your obnoxious self." Henry was now outside the door laughing. "Come on, let's go and have a beer."

"Henry, just go away." Wade sounded annoyed. "I thought you were leaving."

"I'm not leaving until I get to thank Lucy in person for the dinner."

"Savannah, are you really going to leave us standing out here for the rest of the night?" Wade's voice was huskier now. "Can we please talk face to face?"

"Fine." I got off of the bed slowly, walked over to the door, and unlocked it. "What do you want?" I folded my arms and stared at him. He was so tall and commanding. It was hard for me to keep glaring at him when all I really wanted to do was melt into his arms.

"I think you know what I want." He licked his lips as he stared at me. "But can we go and talk in private?"

"I don't know." I looked back at Lucy, who was now standing up as well. "Will you be okay?"

"She'll be okay with me," Henry said as he strode into the room. "I promise."

"Why do I not trust you?" I shook my head as he walked over to Lucy.

"I don't know." He grinned at me. "I think I'm a pretty trustworthy guy."

"You can go and talk to Wade, Savannah. I'll be okay." Lucy nodded at me. "We'll chat in the morning?"

"Okay." I nodded back at her. Then I turned back to Wade. "So what do you want to tell me?"

"Why are you so angry with me?" He grabbed my hand and pulled me to him. "You need to talk to me, Savannah."

"Is that a joke? You're the one that needs to talk to me." I tried to pull away from him. "You're the one with all the secrets."

"Come with me." Still holding onto my hand, he led me to his bedroom. He shut the door, locked it, then pushed me back against it and held my hands up. "You're so fucking sexy when you're angry."

I swallowed hard as he gazed down at me. "I thought you said we were going to talk."

"We can talk after."

"After what?"

"After we make love." His fingers ran down the side of my body. "Do you know how badly I want you right now?"

I gasped as he lifted the hem of my skirt up. "Wade … stop." His fingers gripped my ass cheeks as he kissed the side of my neck.

"I want to be inside of you right now," he whispered into my ear. "I want to feel you coming on my cock. I want to see your lips trembling as I bring you to orgasm. I want to watch your face as you ride me." He growled as his lips moved closer to mine. "And then I want to take your other cherry." His fingers moved down the crack of my ass and I jumped. He chuckled then and bit down on my lower lip. "I want to fill you up everywhere, Savannah."

"That's not going to happen." I shook my head vehemently. "No way am I letting you inside my ass."

"Are you scared?" He laughed as he ground his cock into my stomach. "Trust me, my big fat cock won't hurt you. I'd take it slow."

"*Not* going to happen."

"I have lube."

"Are you not understanding the words that are coming out of my mouth?" I shivered as he kissed the side of my neck.

"I understand, but you don't know what I'm missing." He chuckled. "You drive me crazy, Savannah."

"You drive me crazier, Wade Hart." I sighed. "But I want some answers. I have some questions and you need to answer them. I'm not sleeping with you again."

"Never?" He raised an eyebrow.

"We'll see."

He stepped back. "Let's go for a swim and then talk?"

"I think we need to talk and then swim."

"Fine, but only on one condition."

"What condition?"

"We skinny dip." He grinned wickedly. "I say that's a fair compromise."

"Waade!"

"Savaaannah!" He teased back.

"Fine, but if I don't get the answers I want, then I'm done."

"Fine." He nodded and grinned. "Now come on, the pool is calling us."

"Let's grab some towels first." I laughed as he ran and grabbed two towels, while at the same time pulling off his shirt.

CHAPTER 17

"I'm going to do something for you, Savannah." Wade did a little dance next to the pool.

I laughed. "What's that?"

"I'm going to do a striptease for you."

"A striptease?" I licked my lips. "Really?"

"Really. Didn't you enjoy the movie *Magic Mike?*"

"Are you telling me you're like Channing Tatum?"

"I'm better, baby." He started undoing his shirt and dancing around in front of me. He pulled his shirt off and threw it onto the ground. He walked over to me and flexed his pecs. I giggled as I reached out to touch him but he danced out of my reach. "No touching the goods, baby."

"Oh?"

"Not yet." He winked and stepped back and unbuckled his belt. He pulled it off and dropped it to the ground, then slowly unzipped his pants. I couldn't keep my eyes off of his crotch. The bulge in his briefs as he pulled his pants off was massive. "Like what you see, little lady?" He danced around me, and I could feel my skin warming up.

I turned to look at him as he ran his hands down my back. "Why did you leave me and go hunting that morning?"

Wade stopped dancing. "So, the questions are starting already?"

"Yes, and I want the truth."

"I left because I was overwhelmed." He pulled me towards one of the loungers and sat down.

"Why were you overwhelmed?"

"Because I'd just taken your virginity," he said bluntly, his hands on my thigh. "Take your dress off."

"Not yet." I shook my head. "Explain further, please."

"I was overwhelmed because it was more than just sex, and I didn't know how I felt about that." He grabbed my hand and placed it on his bulge. "You make me horny. My whole body wants you."

"So what's wrong with that?"

"Because this is about more than sex," he said again, his voice soft. "We both know that."

"So, what's wrong about that?"

"It can't be more than sex …" He groaned as I squeezed his cock gently.

"Why not?" I leaned back and watched him through veiled eyes.

"Because it can't."

"Answer me, Wade."

"Will you take your dress off if I do?"

"Yes." I ran my fingers down his chest. "I will."

"I have a past, Savannah." His eyes looked dark as he stared at me. "Things that I can't tell you. And it's not safe for me to get any closer to you."

"But you can sleep with me?" My anger and frustration were clear in my voice.

"I like you, Savannah." He let out a deep sigh. "I really

like you. If I was a different person, maybe this could be more, but, it just can't."

"So I'm just meant to sleep with you and accept that?"

"I can understand why you might not want to." He nodded. "If you want to just end it all here, we can do that."

"Is that what you want?"

"No." He grabbed my hand. "I never want to let you go."

"But you want me to leave."

"I can't always have what I want." He shrugged. "I have a family to protect. I have people all over the world that are counting on me."

"But what about me?"

"I want to love you, Savannah." His tone was sad. "I wish I could love you and offer you a life." He ran his finger down my neck. "I wish."

"But you won't tell me why you can't?"

"No." He shook his head.

"Fine." I looked away from him. I didn't even care what it was that he was hiding now. I was too hurt that he didn't trust me enough to tell me. It broke me that he knew we had something special but didn't want to give us a chance. He didn't care about me enough to actually want something real with me.

"You're sad." His voice was soft. "I didn't want to make you sad." He shifted closer to me and pulled me into his arms. "Don't be mad at me."

"I'm not mad at you." I looked up into his eyes. "I just don't understand what's going on."

"I know." He held my face in his hands and he gazed at me with a passionate gaze. "She walks in beauty, like the night

Of cloudless climes and starry skies;

And all that's best of dark and bright

Meet in her aspect and her eyes;

Thus mellowed to that tender light
Which heaven to gaudy day denies."

"When I look at you, I think of that poem."

"I have to admit that I'm shocked you can recite Lord Byron."

There was a moment of silence when he was done. H cleared his throat. "'She Walks in Beauty' has always been one of my favorite poems." His eyes never left mine. "And how appropriate to recite it to the most beautiful woman I've ever met."

"Whatever." I blushed, though I loved hearing him saying that. If I hadn't known I loved him before, I surely did now.

"When I die, it will be your face I see before me."

"Wade," I shook my head and laughed. "You're an idiot."

"Am I?"

"Yes."

I stood up and pulled my dress off slowly. I loved the look of lust on his face as I stood there in my bra and panties. I unhooked my bra and let it fall to the ground, relishing his sharp intake of breath as my fingers fell to my panties and slowly pulled them off.

"You're beautiful," he groaned, staring at my naked body. "I want you so badly, Savannah."

"Then come and get me." I flashed him an evil smile before I ran away from him and dived into the pool. The cold of the water shocked my system as I swam, but I felt so alive as I finally came up for air. Seconds after I surfaced, I felt Wade behind me pulling me into his arms.

"I caught you." He kissed my lips and pressed his body into mine, his cock twitching against my leg. I wrapped my arms around his neck and kissed him back.

"You got those briefs off quickly."

He tugged gently on my wet hair. "I can move quickly if I need to."

He swam me over to the side of the pool where he leaned back against the wall and ran his fingers down my naked breasts. I moaned as his hand slipped between my legs to rub my clit.

Heat, liquid and intense, spread through me. I arched my head back. The water made everything feel so much more sensual. Wade touched me as if he couldn't get enough of me. Suddenly he pulled me back up to him and started kissing me. I kissed him back and reached my hand down to stroke his penis. He groaned against my lips as I ran my fingers back and forth along the length of him. I pushed back and jumped down into the water, holding onto his torso as my lips found his cock. I took him into my mouth underwater and sucked on him as best as I could before going back up for air.

"I want you so badly," he groaned as he pulled me up and I wrapped my legs around his waist. "I wish you were on the pill." He rubbed his cock against my clit and I could feel myself getting even hornier. "I want to fuck you right here."

"That would feel so good," I whispered against his ear. "I wish I could feel your hard cock inside me right now."

"Fuck, Savannah." He groaned at my words as I ground my pussy against him. "You're going to make me lose it."

"I don't want you to lose it." I laughed.

"You tease." His lips crashed down on mine again.

I kissed him back and ran my fingers through his hair. We made out in the pool for what felt like ages, but as he adjusted me on him again, we both knew we had to get out of the water. The tip of his cock was next to my pussy and I knew that if I just moved slightly, he would be inside of me and neither of us would be able to stop.

"Come on," he grunted as he pulled himself out of the

pool. "We need to stop now." He helped me out of the pool and then picked me up.

"What are you doing?" I gasped as he carried me over to the lounger.

"This."

He lay me down and pushed me back. Pushing open my thighs, he dropped his head between them. He took my clit into his mouth, and I cried out as he sucked me, first tenderly and then roughly. His tongue licked up the water between my folds and then entered me as deftly as if it were his cock. My thighs closed in on his head and I held him down as he made love to me with his tongue.

"Oh, Wade!" I cried out, coming hard. "Oh, Wade!"

He licked up my juices eagerly before kissing up my body to my lips.

"I love the way you taste," he groaned as he stroked my breasts. "I'm so fucking hard right now."

"I know." I grinned. "It's my turn now." I pushed him back and ran my fingers to his cock as I moved down the lounger.

"Wait." He grabbed my hand.

"What?"

"I want to pleasure you again."

"What?"

"Sit on my face as you suck me off." He pulled me on top of him. "I want to feel your pussy coming on my mouth as I blow into yours."

"Okay."

I positioned myself over him, whimpering as he pulled me down onto his face, his tongue licking my clit. I shifted position, trembling, then leaned down and took his cock into my mouth. He groaned against my pussy as I got to work. I closed in my lips on him, and soon we were both moving in harmony, pleasuring each other as much as we could. I was close to coming again, so I increased the pressure of my lips on his tip. I didn't want to come again before he'd come. But as he pulled my ass down and ground my pussy against his face, I couldn't hold back. I moved back and forth on his face, then just as I was about to come, his cock stilled and then twitched uncontrollably as he came. I swallowed his cum and screamed as I came once again. I lay there for a few seconds after we'd both come and then scrambled around so that we were face to face again. He pulled me into his arms and kissed me on the lips.

"That was fucking hot." He caressed the side of my face. "And now we need to go to my room because I need to fuck you hard with my cock."

"Wade." I shook my head and reached down to touch his abdomen. I was shocked to feel that he was already growing hard again. "You're insatiable."

"When it comes to you, I am definitely insatiable." He helped me to my feet. I looked around for a towel to wrap myself in, but the towels were both gone. "What's wrong?"

"The towels are gone." I looked around, shivering. "They're gone."

"How can they be gone?"

"I don't know, Wade, but they're gone." My eyes were wide. "Who took the towels?"

"Maybe Henry played a joke on us." Wade's lips thinned. "I'll tell him off."

"So, he was *watching* us?"

"I don't think he would do that ..." Wade sounded angry. "It was a bad joke. I will take care of it."

"But what if it wasn't him?" I whispered. "What if it's the person that's been coming to the house ..." I thought of Gordon. Was he stalking me and Wade?

"Don't worry, Savannah." He wrapped his arms around

me. "I'll figure it out, okay? Come with me." He grabbed his shirt and handed it to me. "Put this on, and we'll go inside."

"Okay."

I pulled his shirt on while he picked up the rest of our clothes, then Wade grabbed my hand and led me inside. In silence, we walked to his room, where he locked the door behind us then turned to me. Swooping me up into his arms, he carried me to the bed. Pulling out a condom, he slipped it on and then lay down on the bed as well. Nudging my legs open with his knee, he positioned himself on top of me and entered me with one deep thrust.

I cried out, raking my fingers ran down his back. He fucked me hard and fast, neither one of us saying a word. My orgasm built up until he reached his fingers down to my clit and I exploded immediately, gasping and shuddering. Then he suddenly pulled out of me, slipped the condom off, and came all over my stomach. We lay there in each other's arms for a few minutes, his cum drying on our skin as he kissed the side of my neck.

"Give me five more minutes and then we can go again," he whispered into my ear. "And this time, you're going to be on top." I ran my fingers across his lips and just nodded, still unable to speak. "And maybe you'll even let me inside your ass," he teased me as he sucked on my finger. I just moaned in response. This man could say whatever he wanted to me. I was too far gone to say no to him. I just had to make sure that he didn't know that.

If he wasn't ready to share all of himself with me, I wasn't ready to give all of myself to him.

CHAPTER 18

My body was aching when I woke up, but it was the pleasant sort of ache that I didn't mind. I rolled over in the bed to look for Wade, but he was gone. My heart lurched as I saw the note on his pillow.

"Not again," I muttered under my breath as I reached for the note. The anxiety drained out of me as I read it. He hadn't disappeared on another "trip." He'd just gone out for the day and would be back for dinner.

I got up and made my way to the bathroom, annoyed that he'd left so early again. I just didn't understand why he did that. Didn't he want to wake up and hug and kiss in the morning, like I did? I enjoyed our lovemaking, but it seemed like every morning after, he disappeared. What happened to sweet kisses and breakfast in bed?

Though knowing Wade, he'd expect me to serve him.

I jumped into the shower and washed quickly. On the bright side, Lucy and I would have the house to ourselves while we looked for the basement. That would make it a lot easier for us to snoop.

Ten minutes later, I was dried and dressed and tapping on Lucy's door.

"Hey, girl, you up?" I stuck my head into the room.

"I've been ready and waiting for an hour." She jumped up off of the bed. "Good night?"

"It was okay …" I stared at her suspiciously. "Why are you so chipper? What went down last night with you and Henry?"

"Nothing went down, unfortunately." She made a face. "Though I did get a little kiss."

"You kissed him?"

"Well, he kissed me. I didn't stop him."

"Oh, Lucy, I hope you tell me a bit more later." I giggled. "What do you want for breakfast?"

"Are you cooking or are we going to the diner?"

"I'm cooking."

"Then I'll have a boiled egg and some toast, please."

"You have no faith in my cooking skills." I made a face as we walked to the kitchen.

Lucy just laughed. "Where's Wade?"

"He's gone out." I shrugged. "I don't know where, but he said he won't be back until tonight."

"Awesome!" Lucy did a little dance next to the counter. "I think the first thing we should do is look for the basement and see what's down there."

"Yeah, that's what I was thinking, though I have no idea where it could be."

"Did you see where Wade went when he went to get the wine?"

"Nope." I shook my head. "I wasn't really paying attention."

"Yeah, me either." She sighed. "But not to worry, I have faith in us. We will find it."

"I sure hope so." I opened the fridge and took out four

eggs. "I just hope we don't find something horrible hidden down there."

⚜

"We have searched this house for two hours and nothing." Lucy's voice expressed the frustration that I felt. "How can a basement be hidden this well?"

"I wish I knew." I sighed. "But we've looked absolutely everywhere."

"He obviously doesn't want anyone to find it." Lucy slapped the wall impatiently then reached for her phone to check it. "So what do we do now?"

"I don't know." I was out of ideas. "How about we go to the library? Maybe we can look for some more photos and letters from Wade's mom or dad. Maybe there will be some clues. Or we could ... Lucy, are you listening to me?"

Lucy's eyes were glued to her phone. "Savannah, I think our luck has just changed."

"Why?"

"I just received an email from the New York Public Library with some attachments."

"The articles?"

"It has to be the articles." She nodded. "Let's go to the library. You look through the letters and photos, and I'll go through these articles. You know I'm a speed reader. Let's see what we can figure out."

"Yes, Sherlock."

As soon as we got to the library, Lucy immediately sat down at the desk and I walked over to the stacks of books that I'd found photos and letters in before. I grabbed some of the books and started leafing through them, not really knowing what I was hoping to find. The books were empty, and I put them down quickly. I was putting back one particularly heavy book when a piece of paper slipped out of the bottom.

"Oh shit, how did I miss that?" I murmured as I carefully pulled the paper out of the book and walked over to the table.

"Did you find something?"

"Looks like a letter, but I don't know if it will be helpful. How are the articles going?"

"They're interesting, very interesting." She looked up, pen in her mouth.

"Are you going to tell me more?"

"Read the letter. We'll talk later." She shook her head. "Now shh, I need to read."

"Fine." I took a seat and read the letter. It was from Joseph Hart, Wade's dad, and once again I felt like I was intruding on someone's personal thoughts. I could feel myself choking up as I reread the letter. It felt so raw and my heart broke for Joseph, Wade, and Henry. "Lucy, you have to hear this. I found something interesting."

"So did I." Lucy's eyes were lit up with excitement. "But you go first. What's it about?"

"It's a letter from Wade's dad to his mom."

"Oh?"

"Yeah, listen to this. 'To my darling Louisa, my heart beats only for you. I was staring at the stars last night and I saw a shooting star. I stopped and I watched it and I realized the last shooting star I saw was with you when we were in Australia. I love you, my dear. I miss you. Forgive me. Please forgive me. I cannot go on without you in my life. I feel like a fawn that has lost its mother and is living in the woods alone. The loneliness is unbearable. I need you more than I need air. Return to me. Come home. Save me or I shall surely die.'"

"Oh, wow." Lucy's misty-eyed expression suddenly vanished and she sat up straight. "Oh, wow!"

"What?"

"So, the articles I found, I think they might relate to that letter."

"How?"

"Do you know exactly how Wade's dad died?"

"No, why?"

"So get this." She looked at my laptop, surveying the screen again and then continued talking. "He killed himself … and it looks like he did it in front of his sons."

"Oh, no." My hand flew to my face. "That's horrible."

"Supposedly, he jumped off a cliff into a waterfall and hit his head on a rock, but …"

"But what?"

"His body was never found."

"Okay …"

"Yeah and get this, there was a reporter who wondered if Joseph Hart was actually murdered … *by one of his sons*."

"No way!" My heart started to pound and I felt a little sick.

"Supposedly they'd all had an argument about something, and next thing you know, he was dead."

"Oh, shit."

"And the investigative reporter was Misha Waterman. Remember I told you about her before?"

"Yeah, her name does sound familiar."

"And, Savannah," Lucy's voice dropped. "Don't freak out, but I have something to tell you."

"What?"

"Misha got an undercover job to investigate the possible murder."

"Okay?" The sick feeling was intensifying.

"She got a job as Wade's assistant."

"She was his assistant?" I rubbed my temple. "Where is she now? What happened?"

"She quit her job as a reporter and she is no longer working for that newspaper. I can't find any information for her online. She's not on LinkedIn, she's not on Facebook." Lucy shook her head. "She seems to have just disappeared off the face of the earth."

"Where did she go?"

"Maybe she didn't go anywhere, Savannah. Maybe she's still in this house."

I shivered. "You're scaring me, Lucy."

"What if she found out that Wade killed his dad, and then he killed her? What if she's buried in the basement?"

"No." I shook my head vehemently. "There's no way. Wade is not a killer."

"Savannah, I know you don't want to think he could be a bad guy, but we have to face facts."

"I've slept with him, Lucy. I've looked into his eyes as he's been inside of me. He's not a killer. I know it in my bones."

"You *want* to know it."

"No, I *know* it." I jumped up. "He didn't kill his dad."

"It would all add up, Savannah."

"All we know is that the father died by jumping off a cliff." I shrugged. "There is nothing to indicate that Wade pushed him."

"Maybe he didn't *mean* to kill him but there was a struggle and his dad fell. Or maybe he *did* mean to kill him and disposed of the body."

I rolled my eyes to the ceiling. "You need to stop thinking with your filmmaking brain, Lucy. This isn't a thriller on Lifetime. This is real life. Wade didn't kill his dad. He had no reason to kill his dad."

"Maybe Wade was pissed because he found out that his dad was cheating on his mom. Maybe he was pissed because he realized he didn't have a relationship with her because his father's actions. Or maybe it wasn't on purpose. Maybe it was an accident."

"That's a lot of maybes, Lucy." I shook my head. "It's not possible. Wade could never do such a thing."

"But if he did, and you were to find out and go to the police, that would ruin him, Savannah. He would be jailed. That would be it. You could *destroy his life*." Lucy threw her hands up in the air triumphantly. "It makes sense, Savannah. I feel it in my bones."

"So then we should leave." I crossed my arms. "Let's pack our bags and leave now. If you think he's a murderer, then we need to go."

"What?" Her eyes narrowed. "We can't just leave. We need to figure out what's the truth ..." She sighed. "Okay, fine. So maybe I don't have it down exactly."

"Wade is not a murderer," I said stubbornly. "I don't care what you think. I just know it. Do you also think Henry is hiding the fact that his brother is a murderer? You think he's okay with it?"

"No." She shook her head slowly. "I don't think so."

"So there's more to the story."

"We need to find that reporter. We need to find Mischa."

"How the hell do we find her?"

"I'll call the newspaper tomorrow and see if I can get her contact info. I'll say I'm a headhunter or something."

"Okay."

"And you need to ask Wade again what happened to his assistant and where she went."

"He doesn't know."

"Try. Just be casual about it."

"Ugh, I don't know. That makes me nervous."

"Savannah, don't you want to know the truth."

"I do!" I insisted, though I wasn't entirely sure it was the truth.

"Don't you think it's suspicious that a reporter started to investigate him and the death of his father and now she's just disappeared?"

"We don't know if—"

"Savannah!" Lucy raised her voice.

"Fine, yes, it is a little suspicious," I relented, though I almost felt like a traitor for saying those words. "I will speak to Wade and see if I can get any more information."

"Great. I should do some work." Lucy made a face. "I have a long conference call for work tonight, and I'm totally not prepared."

"I feel ya." I sighed. "I have some documents to transcribe for Wade. And I better do that before he asks me what's going on."

"If he does, you can just kiss him and change the subject."

"Yeah, that's not going to happen. Wade doesn't play when it comes to business."

"He does seem really dedicated to his work." Lucy seemed thoughtful. "Was he working with his dad when the company nearly went bankrupt?"

"Girl, I have no idea." I shrugged. "I don't know him that well."

"Well, remember that." She gave me a knowing look. "You *don't* know him that well, so there are many things that can surprise you."

"You don't like him, do you?"

"Honestly, I see his charm. I get why you've fallen for him. But you're my best friend, and I'm not going to let you go any further down this rabbit hole until we figure out just how mad your hatter is."

"I know. You're a good friend. I guess let's see what happens."

CHAPTER 19

I sat in the backyard with Jolene, my feet hanging over the side of the pool kicking the water around. The sun was going down and my anxiety level was going up. Jolene was lying in the grass, snoring her head off, and Lucy was in the house on her business call. Wade still hadn't come back home and I'd spent the last hour thinking of how I was going to ask him more about Mischa.

While I rejected the idea that Wade could have been involved in his father's death in any way, there was still a small, nagging voice in the back of my mind asking if I was just being blinded by love and good sex.

"Jolene, am I a fool?" I asked my sleeping dog as if I expected an answer from her. "I'm just a fool living in a dreamworld, spending my days dreaming of you," I sang to myself as I splashed. I thought about changing into my swimsuit and having a quick swim, but I didn't want to get my hair wet. I loved swimming, but it was a hassle having to wash it after being in the pool.

I stood up and walked over to Jolene and bent down to stroke her silky hair.

"I've missed you, Jolene." Her eyes fluttered open. She wagged her tail then rolled onto her back so I could rub her belly. I laughed as her mouth fell open and tongue lolled out. "Oh, you love me so much, don't you, Jolene?" I giggled as I continued to rub her, but suddenly she rolled back over and stood up with a shake.

"Am I paying you to play with your mutt?"

I turned around to see a teasing look on Wade's handsome face. He had shaved, and the scruff from his time in the woods was gone. I'd thought primal, primitive Wade had been even sexier than civilized Wade, but now that civilized Wade was back, I wasn't sure anymore. They were both scorching hot.

I blushed at the look he was giving me. I couldn't believe that he had such an affect on my body.

"Her name is Jolene, and I did the work you left for me."

Wade crouched down and rubbed Jolene's head. "Why'd you name her Jolene?"

"After the Dolly Parton song," I told him. "It was one of my favorites when I was growing up. There was a girl in my high school who would sing it every day, and I guess it just stuck."

"You like country music?"

"Yeah, do you?"

"Nah." He shook his head. "That's not my jam."

"What's your jam?"

"Metal, classic rock, that sort of thing."

"Typical guy music, I guess."

"I'm anything but a typical guy." He leaned forward and gave me a quick kiss on the lips. "I forgot to greet you properly."

"Properly?"

"With a kiss. Isn't that what you women like?"

"What we women like?"

"You know, to be shown attention from your men."

"You're my boss, not my man."

"Well, last night when I was inside of you, I was your man."

"You're gross, Wade."

"You didn't think that when you were sucking my cock."

"Wade!" I smacked him in the arm. "Stop."

"You're blushing." He chuckled. "I love seeing you blush."

"So, where were you today?" I asked him, trying to ignore the butterflies in my stomach.

"I had to run some errands with Henry." He wrapped his arm around my waist and pulled me into him. "What did you do?"

"I was working." I pressed my face into his chest. I didn't want him to see that I was lying, but I wasn't about to say, *I just was looking for your basement to see if I could find a dead body. Oh, and Lucy and I snooped all through your house to figure out your secrets.*

"Savannah?" He kissed the top of my head. "What are you thinking about?"

"Nothing." I looked up into his eyes and stood up on my tippy toes so that I could kiss him. "I'm glad you're home," I said honestly, and I realized just how true those words were. I was never happier than when I was spending time with him.

"Do you trust me?" he asked me. His voice was soft, and his eyes were shining.

"Why?" I swallowed hard. Was he about to tell me his secrets? Was this all going to be over?

"Because I want to try something with you. I know you'll enjoy it, but you have to relax."

"Wade Hart, I am not having anal sex with you!" I snapped, covering my disappointment with annoyance. He was asking me if I trusted him because he wanted to have kinky sex with him, not because he was falling for me and wanting to share his deepest, darkest secrets with me.

"Did I say anal?" He raised an eyebrow.

"Then what are you talking about?"

"I'll tell you if you say yes."

"I'm not saying yes if I don't know what I'm saying yes to."

"Then we're in a bit of a conundrum, aren't we?"

"We're not. *You* are."

"Touché." He laughed and stepped back. "Would you like to go on a walk tonight?"

"A walk where?"

"Does it matter?"

"Kinda."

"What if I said it was somewhere over the rainbow?"

"You're in a weird mood." My eyes narrowed at how light-hearted and goofy he was being. "What's going on?'

"Does something have to be going on for me to want to take a walk with my best gal?"

"Your best gal?" Despite myself, my heart fluttered at his words. "What does that mean?"

"I don't know." He took my hand. "What can I say? It's been a long time since I wooed someone."

"Are you wooing me?"

"Can you woo your assistant?"

"I don't even know if you can woo, period. It's 2020." I laughed, even though I loved the way his warm fingers entangled with mine.

"Maybe I'm an old-fashioned man."

"You don't strike me as one." Even as I spoke, a voice in the back of my head was telling me to ask him about Mischa. I tried to resist it, but I knew that I couldn't do that for long.

"Well, there are a lot of things you don't know about me,

Savannah." His lips were smiling, but the sparkle in his eyes had dimmed and his expression was inscrutable.

"Then why don't you start telling me more?" I knew I had to tread carefully with this line of questioning. I couldn't just come out and say, *Did you kill your dad? Did you kill your assistant? Am I in danger?*

"What do you want to know? I'm pretty much an open book."

"You, an open book?" I laughed. "That's a joke, right?"

"Would I joke about such a thing?"

"Yes." I rolled my eyes at him. "When you're not trying to boss me around, you're trying to sleep with me, and you're cagey and sarcastic as hell. I wouldn't say you're an open book. You don't really let me in. Not that I expect to be let in, as I'm only your assistant."

"Obviously, you're not just my assistant. You know that, right?"

"Well, what am I?"

"I don't know exactly, but we're more than just employer and employee."

"Obviously." I snorted.

"Shall we go inside and have a drink and then we can talk a bit—"

"What happened to Mischa, your last assistant?" I blurted out, unable to stop myself.

He stiffened. "What do you mean? How'd you know her name?"

"Don't deflect. What exactly happened when she worked here?" I folded my arms and held my chin up. *Smooth Savannah, real smooth.*

"She was very nosey." He answered with a slight edge in his voice. "I found her snooping in my office, going through files she had no business going through, and so I fired her."

"You fired her?"

"Yes."

"And where did she go?"

"Back home?" He shrugged. "I have no idea. Why?"

"Why don't you have any other help in this house? It's a huge house, and you obviously have the money."

"I don't need other help." His lips thinned. "I prefer to have my space and not deal with too many people on my property."

"In case they go snooping?"

"Would you like someone snooping in your house?"

"Obviously not." I took a deep breath. I wasn't getting the answers I needed so I had to keep going, harder and deeper. "Did you know she was a reporter?"

"Who was a reporter?" His eyes narrowed as he studied my face. My face grew hot under his scrutiny.

"Mischa was, and she was investigating you."

Wade frown deepened. "And you know this how?"

"I wanted to find out more about the man I was working for."

"So you started stalking me?"

"Googling someone isn't stalking them."

His jaw tightened. "You can't find out that information on Google. I know what exists on the web about me. You obviously had other means of investigating me." He shook his head angrily. "Fuck it, Savannah."

"Why are you so upset? What happened to her?"

"I already told you I have no idea."

"You know she quit the paper and hasn't been heard from since she was working here." I embellished the last part. I had no idea if she'd been heard from or not, but I wanted to see if I could trip him up.

"How would I know that?" he growled. "Do you think I did something to her?"

"Did you?" I pointed at him. "What are you hiding,

Wade? Where is she?"

"Why don't you ask her boyfriend? She was dating some local guy that she met in the village."

"I-I didn't know she had a boyfriend," I stammered, taken aback. "He lives in the village?"

"Yeah, all I know is that his name is Ramsay. If you want to know what happened to her, ask him." He turned away from me and started walking away.

"Where are you going?" I rushed after him.

"Inside."

"Are we still having that drink?"

"I don't think so." He didn't bother meeting my gaze.

"What about that walk?" I asked, alarmed. It was as if he had completely shut down. Why had I pushed everything and been so accusing?

"If you want to go on a walk, don't let me stop you."

"Wade." I reached for his arm. "Don't be mad at me. I was just curious."

He pulled his arm away from me. "I'm going to the office. I have some work to do. I won't be in bed until late tonight."

"Okay." I nodded. "Is there anything you want me to do?"

"No. I think you've done enough."

And with that he was gone, walking back into the house without looking back. How had things gone so bad so quickly? I reached down and rubbed Jolene's head, but even she looked like she was fed up with me.

CHAPTER 20

"Savannah, his reaction seemed extreme."

Lucy unbuckled her seatbelt as I parked outside the Herne Hill Village Cafe. I had told Lucy everything that Wade had told me the evening before, and we'd decided to visit the cafe to ask Beryl if she knew who Ramsay was. If we could talk to Ramsay and then to Mischa, we might finally get to the bottom of this whole mess.

"I know, but he ignored me all night, and he was gone when I woke up this morning."

"He's so moody." She grimaced. "He's really starting to get on my nerves."

"I just feel like shit because I think he was really trying last night. He was being sweet and flirty. And I ruined it all."

"Girl, if you asking a few questions ruined everything, then you didn't have much to ruin in the first place." Lucy looked at me apologetically. "Sorry, but you know it's true."

"I feel like we were getting closer to being boyfriend and girlfriend," I said softly. "This is why you should never sleep with someone you're not actually in a relationship with. It's too hard emotionally."

"I know, girl."

Lucy and I got out of the car and I locked the doors. As we walked toward the café, my heart rate began to pick up. What were we going to find out now?

I checked my phone to see if Wade had texted me, but of course there was nothing from him. I knew that Lucy was right; he was overreacting. Everyone googled and looked people up, especially people they worked for, and most people just accepted that. They didn't just stop talking to people.

"Don't obsess, Savannah. Maybe it's for the best. If he's an asshole, you don't want to end up falling for him even harder."

"I know, I know." I sighed and then took a deep breath as we approached the door. "Well, here we go."

"Do you want me to talk or —"

"I'll talk. I need to take control of this now."

And I knew that I did. Lucy was a good friend and great emotional support, but this was on me. I need to put on my big girl boots and figure this out for myself. I was in love with Wade, I had given myself to him, and I wanted nothing more than to just enjoy my time with him. But I also knew that we couldn't go any further if I was questioning who he was. And as long as he was holding his deep dark secrets, I was never going to know if he was the man I truly believed him to be or if he were someone capable of really dark things.

❧

"Hello, Beryl, I need to ask you some questions," I said as soon as the waitress approached us. Normally I would have ordered something and been more coy, but this was too important. I was hoping that once Beryl provided us some information on Ramsay, then Lucy and I could go and search for him. We didn't have time to sit around and wait for Beryl to come and talk to us.

Beryl's eyes filled with apprehension. "Would you like a table?" I shook my head. "I see. Well, come to the counter, and I'll see if I can help."

"Thank you." We all walked over to the counter and I immediately turned to Beryl. "Do you know a guy in the village called Ramsay?"

"Ramsay?" Beryl's eyes narrowed. "No."

"He was dating Wade's last assistant, Mischa. Maybe you remember meeting her?"

"The last girl." Her lips pursed. "Yes, I remember her."

"Do you remember who her boyfriend was?"

"She was always with the Hart boy." She shook her head. "Bad apple."

"Which Hart boy?" I asked her. "Please, this is important. We think something may have happened to her. We need to talk to her."

"You're getting too close." Beryl shook her head. "You should leave, Savannah. You shouldn't get messed up in the Hart mess."

"What do you know, Beryl? Please tell me."

"This is a small village." Her voice got lower. "My husband hunts, you know."

"No, I didn't know." What did that have to do with anything?

"He sees things." Her lips thinned. "Those Hart men have secrets they don't want let out. All of them."

"What secrets?"

She shook her head. "We don't snitch in this town."

"Can you at least tell me how I can find Ramsay? Please?" I begged. "I need to know. I care about Wade, and I need to know if …" My voice trailed off as it cracked with emotion. I didn't really want to tell her everything, but I needed her to know how important it was for me to get all the information that I could."

"All I can say is that there's more than one master chef in this town." She looked over to the door. "And now I must get back to work. I'm sorry, my dear. I can't help you anymore."

"Okay, thanks," I said despondently as she walked away. "I guess that's it, then." I looked over at Lucy. "We're done."

"We could always go to the library and ask questions," Lucy offered, but she knew that was a long shot. "Are there any classy restaurants in town? Maybe he's a chef?"

"I guess we could check."

Lucy tapped her chin thoughtfully. "What else could her comment have meant? There's more than one master chef in this town?"

"I don't even know one, let alone more than one." I let out a long deep sigh and rubbed my forehead. "Ugh, I'm starting to get a headache."

"I'm so sorry, Savannah." Lucy drew in a deep breath. "I think we should leave."

"Why?"

"She basically told us that Henry or Wade was dating Mischa, and her husband saw one of them killing her in the forest. It all adds up." Lucy bit her lip. "Girl, think about it. She didn't want to say it outright, but she basically told us."

"I was wondering why she was telling us her husband likes hunting."

"Savannah, she told us that he saw something. It's all adding up." Lucy shivered. "We need to leave tonight. I'm not sure we're safe. Well, I'm not sure that *you're* safe."

"Why do you say that?"

"You said Wade was pissed and then distant at your questioning? What if he's planning something?"

"What do you mean? Planning what?"

Lucy's lips thinned. "Not your engagement, that's for sure. We need to go home, pack, take Jolene on one last walk, and then leave. Let me look up train times back to the city."

"So we're just going to leave?" My stomach dropped. Was I never going to see Wade again?

"I think that's for the best." Lucy nodded. "I think we need to get out while we still can. We're not going to get any concrete answers, I don't think." She shook her head. "And we have to be okay with that."

"You don't think there's anything else we can do?"

"Not really, not unless we speak to Gordon. Maybe he has more information."

"Let me try him one last time."

I called him as we made our way back to the car, but as the call went to voicemail, I realized that it was all over. Gordon was deliberately ignoring me. I didn't expect to hear from him again. I was about to hang up when I decided to leave a message, just in case Gordon had a heart.

"Hey, my friend, it's me, Savannah. Haven't heard from you in a while, but I wanted to see how you were doing. I'm okay, though I'm now head over heels in love with Wade. Kill me now, ha ha. So, I have a theory and wanted to talk to you about it. It's important. Please call me back. I miss you. Bye." And then I hung up.

I was hoping that if Gordon cared about me, even a little bit, he would call back and talk to me. And if he did call back, he was going to have to do it in the next few hours because I knew Lucy was right. No matter how much I loved Wade or wanted to believe in him, it wasn't looking good, and if he wasn't going to open up to me at all, I couldn't expect to get any real answers.

The more I was around him, the more I would want him,

and I couldn't allow myself to fall for him any more. I wasn't going to stay with someone who didn't trust me enough to let me into his life.

CHAPTER 21

Lucy and I conceived a plan in case Wade was back home. She would go to her room and pack up all of our stuff while I talked to Wade and did some work. This way, he would be distracted and not realize that something was going on. Then Lucy and I would say we were going to the pub for open mic night and instead catch the train. My heart ached at the thought of leaving Wade, but there was nothing else I could do at this point.

"Savannah, come to the office," Wade called out to me as soon as Lucy and I walked back into the house.

"Yes, sir!" I shouted back to him.

"I'm going to go and pack now," Lucy whispered to me. "Don't forget we have to leave by five. The train leaves at six."

"I know. I'm on it." I nodded and headed to the office. I walked inside and towards Wade's desk. "You called, *sir?*"

"Knock it off, Savannah." He stood up. "You have no idea what it means to call me sir."

"What does that mean?" Butterflies trembled in my stomach as he came towards me.

"It means you have no idea how to be subservient or to listen and do what you're told."

"I always do what I'm told."

"Then go and close the door."

"Why?"

"You don't get to ask why."

"Fine." I walked back and closed the door.

"Lock it," he commanded.

I locked it, my heart pounding. I had a feeling I knew where this was going and I knew I couldn't resist. At least I could have him one last time. This time I would remember every single touch, lick, and kiss ... because this would be the last time.

"Walk over to me." His eyes were filled with lust

Slowly, I walked back to him.

"Drop to your knees."

I was about to protest but I didn't. Instead I fell to my knees and looked up at him with wide eyes.

"Unzip me."

I pulled his zipper down slowly and then pulled his hardening cock out. He gasped at the touch of my fingers on him.

"I didn't tell you to do that."

"Sue me."

"Take me into your mouth and don't stop sucking until I tell you to," he growled as his cock nudged my lips. I opened my mouth as wide as I could and pressed my lips against his shaft, taking him as deep into my mouth as I could without gagging. He grunted as I sucked and licked. I increased my pace.

"Keep sucking my cock," he muttered as his hands came down to my head. "Fuck, yeah, I'm going to come in your mouth." He moved his hips in rhythm to my movements so that it was like he was fucking my face. I held onto his legs as he went deeper and deeper until suddenly his body was shuddering and he was exploding in my mouth. I swallowed his salty juices, strangely enjoying his taste.

Finally he pulled his cock out. "Stand up," he ordered. I stood. "Kiss me." I leaned forward and pressed my lips against his. His tongue entered my mouth and he grabbed my hair and pulled as we kissed. His hand slid to my breast and squeezed. I moaned against him.

"I'm still angry with you," he whispered against my lips.

"I'm still angry with you, too." *So angry I'm going to leave, but you don't need to know that.*

"Get on your knees." He pulled away from me.

"Again?"

He raised an eyebrow. "Knees on the floor *now.*"

"Fine." I got to my knees and looked up at him. "Now what?"

"Turn around and get onto all fours."

"All fours?"

"Stick your ass in the air."

My eyes widened as I placed my hands on the ground as well. He knelt onto the ground behind me and pulled my pants down, exposing my ass to the naked air.

"Oh!" I leaned forward as I was about to lose my balance. I felt his fingers between my legs, and he groaned as he rubbed my wetness.

"So wet and willing. You want my cock inside of you, don't you?"

"Yes," I whispered. I wasn't going to bother lying. This was our last time together. I didn't care if it was an angry fuck. I just wanted him inside of me. I wanted to feel him one last time.

"You want this?" He slipped a finger inside of me as his thumb rubbed my clit and my body crumpled.

"Yes!" I cried out as his finger slid in and out of me.

"Ohhhh, yes!"

"Or do you want this?" He slipped his finger out and pushed the tip of his cock next to my clit and rubbed back and forth.

"Wade," I moaned, shocked that he was hard again already.

"You're glistening for me," he moaned. "Lean forward and put your ass higher in the air."

I shifted my upper body towards the floor and then cried out as he shifted me back towards him. His erection slid between my folds and rubbed against me, and all I wanted was to feel him inside of me.

"Please, Wade."

"Please what?"

"Please fuck me."

He growled at my words and I felt his cock slipping inside of me in one excruciatingly slow movement until he was fully inside of me, filling me up completely. And then he slid out.

"I need to get a rubber," he muttered before sliding back into me, this time faster and with more intent.

"Wade ..." I groaned. "Please."

"Your pussy feels so good on my cock." He pounded a few strokes into me and then pulled all the way out. "Hold on." He stood up and walked over to the side of the room. "I would love to fuck you with no protection, but it's not smart. You need to get on the pill."

I didn't answer him. I didn't need to get on the pill because this was the last time I'd be having sex with him. I heard him rip open a condom wrapper and then he was behind me again. This time, there was no gentleness to his movements. He grabbed my hips and thrust into me hard. He pounded me from behind and my eyes fluttered as his tip hit my g-spot.

This position seemed to allow him to fill me even more than usual and I was completely overwhelmed by the feel of him as he slammed in and out of me. He reached under my abdomen and started to rub me at the same time and in no time, I was screaming out his name as I came harder and with more force than I ever had before. He grunted in satisfaction as he came minutes later, slamming harder than ever before as he exploded once again. He pulled out of me and stood up.

"Get up," he barked as I lay there, completely exhausted. I pulled my pants back up and stood up. "Go and shower and put on a dress with no underwear and come back. I have a plan for the night."

"I told Lucy I'd take her to the pub."

"Tonight?" His expression darkened showing his disapproval.

"Yes, tonight."

"Fine, I'll wait up." His eyes crinkled. "What I have planned can wait."

"What do you have planned?"

"You'll see." He winked. "Go and shower and I'll see you later."

"Okay," I nodded, still dazed from the intensity of my orgasm.

"Come here." He pulled me towards him and kissed me softly. "I do like you, Savannah. Sometimes I think I might feel more than like, but it's complicated …" His voice trailed off and he sighed. "Well, that's enough for now. Go."

He gave me one last kiss and pushed me away. I didn't respond to his comments. It was too late. It was over.

I walked towards the door feeling the saddest I'd ever felt in my entire life. Leaving was hard enough, but having to leave without even a goodbye was much harder.

CHAPTER 22

"Gordon called me!" I hurried to the bedroom to talk to Lucy after my shower. "He wants to meet up with me and chat, right now!"

"Now?" She frowned. "But we're leaving soon."

"I have to go. I need some answers."

"Can't he talk to you on the phone?"

"No, he said he wants to talk in person. He's going to pick me up in a few minutes. He wants to take me somewhere."

Lucy's eyes filled with apprehension. "Savannah, I don't like this."

"It will be okay, Lucy. I promise. It will all be okay."

"I just want us to leave." She shivered. "I'm scared. I really get the creeps being here."

"Have all the bags ready, and we will leave as soon as I get back, okay?"

"I don't like it, but fine." She sighed. "I will text you to check in on you, okay?"

"Sure. I won't be long. I'm going to go to the front and

walk to the end of the driveway so that Wade doesn't see Gordon's car."

"Okay." Lucy nodded. "Good luck."

"Thanks, girl." I gave her a quick hug and then hurried out of the room before she could convince me that it wasn't a good idea.

☙❦❧

"Thanks for meeting me." Gordon's face looked drawn and tired.

I got into the passenger's seat of Gordon's car and shut the door. "I was happy to hear from you. I thought you were ignoring me."

"I was." He pressed his foot on the gas and peeled out of the driveway. "But then I heard your message and figured I owed it to you to meet up."

"I know you're mad with me, but you can't just snoop in someone else's house."

"It should be my house as well!" he shouted, hitting the steering wheel.

Startled, I looked over at him and wondered if he was all right to drive. I'd never seen him like this before. "What do you mean?"

"I was his son too!" Gordon took a corner a little faster than necessary. "I should have been one of the beneficiaries of his will!"

"Joseph Hart?" I said softly. So I'd been right. He was Wade's half brother.

"Yes, Joseph Hart was my dad as well. Not that he cared. Wade is my brother." Gordon sounded angry. "My own flesh and blood, and he doesn't even know or care."

"But why don't you just go and talk to him? Why don't you explain?" I asked.

"I'm waiting for the right opportunity, plus I want to find out the real story behind my father's death. He wasn't that old."

"Oh?" I stared at him. "Do you think someone did something to him?"

"There was talk that he didn't kill himself, yes."

"Did you know Mischa, Wade's assistant, well?"

"No." He pressed down even harder on the gas. "Why?"

My phone beeped at that moment, and I pulled it out of my handbag. There was a text from Lucy.

Come home!! Gordon is the one!! I was googling Master Chef's in Herne Hill Village, and the TV show came up. Guess who the host of the show is??

"Gordon Ramsay," I said under my breath without even having to read the rest of her message. So Gordon was lying. Gordon knew Mischa very well. Was he the one who had made her disappear? My blood went cold.

"I know you're lying, Gordon," I said softly. "I know you're not gay. You're a good actor, but I know Mischa was your girlfriend."

"You know?" He looked at me, his eyes dark and crazed. He nodded to himself. "You know. How?"

"It doesn't matter." I shook my head. "Where is she, Gordon? What happened to her?"

"What happened to her?" He laughed hysterically. "She left me."

"What?" Was he telling the truth?

"She thought I was obsessed with finding out what happened with the Harts and my dad. I was the one that gave her the information to write those articles. No one wanted to take it seriously, but I know something shady went down. I just know it."

"Gordon," I spoke gently. "This doesn't sound healthy. You need to let it go."

"I will never let it go!" The car swerved slightly and I grabbed the side of the door. "Just because you decided to slut it up with Wade, you want to defend him, but he and Henry are scum!"

"How dare you talk to me like that?" I snapped. "You were using me weren't you? You never really cared about being my friend, did you? You just wanted access to Wade. It was all an act!"

"It wasn't an act." Gordon's voice cracked and he looked at me with sad eyes. "Please believe that, Savannah." He sighed. "I'm sorry for calling you a slut."

Gordon blew past a stop sign. He was driving even faster now, and I was getting frightened. "Why are you driving so fast?"

"I'm just trying to get you somewhere. I want to show you something." He turned a corner and slowed down slightly this time. "I know you might not believe me now, but I care about you, Savannah, you're my only real friend."

He was silent for a few seconds and then I heard him sniffling. I tore my gaze away from the road and looked at him. He was crying silent, ugly tears and his body was shaking.

"You don't know what it's like," he sobbed. "My mom had an affair with my dad, and my dad didn't give two shits about either of us. He never even saw me. I called him every year on his birthday, ever since I was ten. I thought he just didn't have my number. I thought he didn't want to see me because he hated my mom, but that wasn't it. He just didn't care. He wasn't interested in meeting me. He didn't care if I was alive or dead. When I was fifteen, I had heart surgery. I thought he'd come. I nearly died, but he didn't even call." The pain in his voice made my heart break. "You forgave Wade for being a jerk to you because he's hurt that his mom treated his dad badly, but he always knew his dad loved him, and he has his brother. I have no one, Savannah. I have no one. My mom died, my dad died, and I was left with nothing. I wanted to meet my brothers. I wanted to belong. I just wanted someone. And I wanted answers."

"Why didn't you try and meet Wade?" I rubbed my arms to stop my body from shaking. "Why didn't you go to his house and tell him you were his brother?"

"Because I didn't want him to think that I was there for money. I never wanted money. I just wanted a family. I just wanted to belong. My whole life …" He stopped then and slammed his fists against the wheel. "You don't understand, I've just never been enough."

"You've been enough to me, Gordon. You've always been enough. You've been a good friend to me. You're friendly, you're talented, *so* talented." I was starting to cry as well. "You could be a huge star. You're one of the best actors I've ever seen. I told you that when we first met."

"It's not enough, don't you get it? I'm not good looking enough, not rich enough, not personable enough. I'm just never enough!" he shouted. "I went to Los Angeles, you know. I don't like to tell people, but I went to the City of Angels. It was full of evil bastards who just wanted to steal your dreams. I never got one callback."

He sounded so sad that I just wanted to pull him into my arms. "I'm sorry, Gordon." His intentions in the beginning may not have been the purest, he hadn't been lying about our friendship; he was just a broken soul. A heartbroken, lost soul. "I believe in you, you know. Don't give up."

"Do you forgive me?" He looked to the side, a look of hope on his face. "Are we still friends?"

"Always! You'll never get rid of me." I smiled and the expression on his face changed into one of absolute happiness. "We're family now, Gordon. Some families we're born into and others we make."

"I love you, Savannah Carter. You're amazing."

He turned to look at me, a smile crossing his tear-stained face, but his eyes were off the road a split second too long. A bright flash of white light poured through the window. A horn blared and something smashed into us.

The car was spun and spun and spun. As we careened towards a group of trees, I pictured my mom and dad playing with me as a child. I'd never doubted their love for me. Then I pictured Lucy, dancing around our living room, singing a Whitney Houston song to me while Jolene stared up at her with wide eyes from her spot under the table. And then I pictured Wade. Tall, masculine Wade with his enigmatic smile and beguiling green eyes, staring into my eyes, kissing my cheek, playing with my hair.

And I knew as I'd known from the very beginning that I loved him. I loved him, and I hoped that he knew just how very much I adored him. For all his flaws, there was nothing I would change about him. Not even his secrets. I didn't want to leave him and I knew that I could forgive him anything. If only I'd have a chance to tell him that. If only I could tell him that he could tell me anything. I'd never judge him. Never.

I heard a scream—I think it was me—then the car slammed into the trees and everything went black. All my worries, questions and concerns were finally gone.

And I was at peace.

CHAPTER 23

Life is made up of moments, and each moment defines who we are. Often, we're distracted, or hurried, or annoyed. Often, we don't realize that one insignificant moment has shaped something momentous. Don't let this moment pass you. Don't let this be just another moment. Love your friends. Love your family. Forgive. Make Peace. Protect your heart and your soul. It all ends too quickly. Far, far too quickly, and then it's too late. Then you're returned to your maker and all you can do is look back.

And when you look back, you want to be able to say, *I lived my life. I loved my life. I cried and I laughed. I had heartache and heartbreak. I had true friends and a true love. And I cared about the humanity of others. For what can be better than that?*

CHAPTER 24

"She's gone."

She's gone? I felt like I was floating, looking down. I could see the hospital room. Was I dead, then? Was that it for me? I lived a good life. A short life, but a good life. I'd known love. Oh, I'd never know love could feel like that.

"She's gone to get some coffee, but she'll be back." The voice was husky. "You should get some sleep, Wade. They say she could still be asleep for a while. She has a severe concussion."

It was Henry talking. Who had gone?

"I'm not leaving until she's up." I recognized Wade's deep voice. My Wade. He was here. He was here. I wanted to look at him, but I couldn't see.

"Shall I text Lucy and tell her to get you some coffee as well?"

"How do you have Lucy's phone number?" Wade sounded suspicious.

"Does that matter right now?"

"No." Wade sighed. "I just need her to wake up. I need to tell her how I feel."

"She's going to be okay, Wade. They said that."

"Then why hasn't she woken up? It's been a week now." He sounded like he wanted to cry. "She has to wake up already."

"She will." Henry shifted to the door. "I'm going to go and help Lucy. I'll be back."

"Okay." Wade didn't look at his brother. He was sitting at the side of a bed where a pale figure lay, hooked up to machines. Wait, was that me? "Savannah Carter, I need you to wake up please. I have some things to tell you." His voice cracked and he started crying. "Please, Savannah."

He was talking to me. I was still floating. Why was I still floating?

"Why did you go with Gordon? Why didn't you tell me? He was my brother. I didn't even know. I knew there was a possibility I had other siblings out there, but I didn't do anything about it. I don't know why. I wish I had looked for him. Welcomed him."

But you can do that now, I wanted to tell him, but my mouth wouldn't open. *You can be a family now.*

"There's nothing like death for you to realize how much you've done wrong in your life," He continued. "I try to be a good man, but I'm selfish. I'm so very selfish."

No. I wanted to hold him to me, but I couldn't make myself reach out to him.

"And now he's gone." Wade's voice cracked again. "He had a stack of letters in his car. Letters to me and Henry, letters to my dad." He took a deep, ragged breath. "He just wanted to be a part of our lives. He was lonely, and I want to hate him for what he did to you, but I can't. I hate myself. This is my fault. This is all my fault. There are too many secrets. Far too many secrets. And I've kept them all."

A white light burned my eyes at his words. Gordon was gone? Gordon was gone! He was dead. Gordon was dead.

We'd crashed. He'd been driving so fast. I remembered now. The fear. The feeling of being hit. Turning and turning and then blackness.

And after the blackness came the light.

"Savannah, I need you to know that I love you. I might even have fallen in love with you before we even met. When you sent me the photo of your dog instead of yourself." He chuckled though his tears. "I knew you were going to be someone special and you were. You are. I love you, Savannah. I know you heard me that night on the phone. I know you heard me talking to Henry telling him you could ruin everything. But it wasn't you that could ruin it. It was me. And I already did." He was sobbing as he spoke. "You didn't deserve to end up with someone like me, a selfish son of a bitch. Oh, Savannah!"

The white was fading now, and my head was throbbing. I wasn't feeling so peaceful any more. I hurt. I hurt all over. My body was aching. I was dead. I was dying. I was going. I was being returned back to where I had come. And all I wanted was to tell Wade I loved him before that happened. To tell him it was okay. That I loved him.

I was crying now, deep inside myself. Crying for me. Crying for Gordon. Crying for Wade. The light was now gone. And now I was back in darkness. Loud beeps screaming in my ear, screaming, screaming.

"Savannah, I love you more than life itself. Come to me, Savannah, come to me." Wade's voice was soothing, talking away the pain and chaos. I was floating back to earth. Floating, floating. "Savannah, don't leave me."

"I won't." My eyes suddenly opened and I stared into his bloodshot eyes. I gave him a weak smile and whispered the words I needed him to hear. "I love you too, Wade, with all my heart.

❧❧❧

"I'm not sure that you're ready to come home yet." Wade frowned as he drove me back to his house. "But I want to take care of you."

"The doctor said it was fine." I yawned, relaxing back into the leather seat. "I was in the hospital for three weeks. I just want to be back home with you."

"I love you." He smiled warmly. "My darling girlfriend."

"Your girlfriend?" I looked over at him. "We never spoke about this."

"I figure you should be my girlfriend before I make you my wife and put a hundred babies into you." He laughed. "Otherwise there might be questions."

"A hundred babies?" I shook my head. "Not going to happen."

"Well, at least fifty, then."

"Why don't we compromise with three?"

"Three works." He grinned. "And we call the first one Gordon."

"He'd like that." A slight sadness filled me as I thought about my friend. "But let's not get carried away, that's not going to happen for a long time."

"I know. We can just enjoy dating for now." He gave me a sly glance. "Maybe now I can convince you to try those things that make you nervous."

"Wade!" He laughed. "But are you ever going to answer my questions?" I asked him. "I still don't know what it is you didn't want me to find out."

The smile faded and he nodded somberly. "All will be revealed when we get home."

"Oh?"

"And I want you to know that whatever you decide to do is okay by me. I'm ready to let this secret out. It's been too long. I don't want it hanging over me anymore, and I don't want it coming between us."

"You're making me nervous."

"I hope you will understand and not judge me too much." He sighed. "I'm not proud of myself, Savannah, but I want to be a better man for you and our future kids."

"What is it, Wade?"

"You'll see."

Wade helped me into the house, my legs shaking with nerves. I froze as we entered the living room and I saw Lucy, Henry and another man sitting at the table. The man had an unkempt beard and long stringy hair and appeared to be in his sixties.

I looked over to Wade, whose face was pale.

"Savannah, I'd like to introduce you to my dad, Joseph Hart."

"What?" My jaw dropped. "But–but—he's dead."

"That's what they thought." The older man stood up, a smile on his face as he approached me. As he got closer, I recognized the familiar green eyes. Wade's dad was alive, but what had happened?

"I need to sit down." I turned to Wade and he walked me over to a chair. We all sat down and I stared at Wade. "What's going on here?"

"It's really quite simple." Wade sighed and shook his head. "My dad was a philanderer and a bad business man. He cheated on my mom and got another woman pregnant, which caused my mom to leave. My dad wanted her back and basically lost control."

His father spoke up. "I made some bad investments. I put the company on the line as collateral. I was going to lose it all, but then I had an idea."

"What idea?" I frowned.

He looked away from me. "I had insurance policies that

would pay out upon my death, and they would save the company. The company that was meant to go to my sons."

"So … you faked your own death?" I turned to Wade. "And you knew? You were in on it?"

"Not originally." Wade shook his head. "Henry and I saw him jump. We thought he'd killed himself. But one summer we went hunting and we found the cabin. He was there."

"We couldn't say anything." Henry spoke up. "It would look like we were a part of the fraud. We'd already collected millions of dollars and reinvested them back into the company. Wade saved the company, but if it came out that our dad was still alive, we knew we'd be prosecuted for fraud. We'd all go to jail." He frowned at his father. "And we weren't even a part of the plan."

"Oh, wow." I nodded though my mind was still blown. Then something occurred to me. "But I think someone else knows …" My eyes were wide. "I think Beryl from the cafe knows. I think her husband saw your dad."

"She knows." Wade sighed. "Do you remember when we went to the cafe and she served us the grilled cheese?"

"Yeah, why?"

"It's my favorite." Joseph grinned. "I always tell Wade to get me the ingredients for grilled cheese when he goes shopping. I could live on them and venison."

"Weird. But that explains the shopping list I found." I rubbed my forehead. "And you trust her not to tell?"

"Beryl was one of the women my dad had an affair with." Wade pursed his lips. "He broke her heart, but she would never betray him."

"Beryl?" I looked at the father. "But isn't she older?"

"Pussy is pussy," Joseph said with a shrug.

Wade glared at him. "That's enough," he growled. "My dad has always danced to the beat of his own drum. He's also the one who was sneaking into the house and taking stuff."

"So it wasn't Gordon?"

"No, it wasn't." Wade squeezed my hand, knowing how guilty I was feeling. "Don't you dare feel bad for suspecting him."

"I'm trying." I took a deep breath. "You thought I'd turn you into the police if I found out? That's why you were worried?"

"A little bit, but I was also falling for you and I didn't want to put you in a compromising position." He rubbed his head. "This information, well, it could get us into trouble and now you know, it puts you in a bad situation as well."

"Oh, Wade." I got up and sat in his lap and kissed him. "I would never turn you in." I didn't even care that everyone was staring at us. "I love you, you goof. I thought you'd killed your dad or something equally horrible. This is nothing. I understand." I wiggled in his lap and he winked as his hardness pressed against my ass.

"Savannah, you do not know how happy that makes me, but I need you to be sure. And if you want me to turn myself in, I will. I will go to jail and do my time. Just promise me, you will wait for me."

"I don't want you to turn yourself in." I shook my head. "You do good work. You're helping people. You're a good man, and that money is helping people." I frowned. "But how come you were able to pay me so much?"

"Because I needed one good person." He kissed me lightly. "And I guess I found her." He wrapped his arms around my waist. "How tired are you?"

"Wade!" Henry rolled his eyes. "Y'all need to go to the bedroom now. And do your thing and we can all talk again later."

"You okay with that?" Wade asked me.

My face hot, I looked over at Lucy, who was grinning. She gave me a small nod.

"Okay," I said softly. Wade lifted me up in his arms as he stood. "You can put me down, Wade, I can walk."

"I'm here to take care of you." He kissed me lightly on the forehead. "This is the beginning of the rest of our lives, and I'm determined to get it right from here on out. I can't lose you again." He began to stride toward the bedroom.

"You didn't lose me, Wade."

"I know you were going to leave that night." He sighed. "I know you were going to catch the train and never look back."

"I would have looked back." I gave him a crooked smile. "I wouldn't have been able to stay away."

"Well, just promise me if you ever feel like you want to leave me again, you'll let me know. I can't live without you in my life, Savannah. You were made for me, and the best thing I ever did was put that ad in that paper."

"Why did you put that ad in the paper? You were such a jerk."

"I had a bet with Henry." He looked a little sheepish. "I bet him that I could hire a woman and get her to do whatever I wanted if I just paid her enough money."

"Wade!" I slapped him in the arm. "How rude! Is that why you were so obnoxious and made me wear that maid's outfit?"

"Yes," he admitted with a wry grin.

"Is that why you slept with me as well?" I looked at him with wide nervous eyes. "Was that part of the bet as well?"

"Never." He shook his head as we walked into the bedroom and he put me down gently on the mattress. "That was all about me, wanting you and needing you." He got on the bed and kissed me. "Kinda like how I feel right now."

"Oh, yeah?" I looked up at his loving expression and smiled. "Well, have at it, big boy. Let's see just how much loving you can give me before I fall asleep."

"Oh, I can give you all the loving." He caressed the side of my face. "And that's what I plan on doing."

"What's that?"

"Giving you all my loving for the rest of my life." His eyes blazed as he gazed down at me. "I love you so much, Savannah Carter, and I'm going to spend an eternity showing you just how deep my love goes."

Thank you for reading Return To Sender. I hope you enjoyed it. Please leave a review if you are able to. Sign up for my mailing list here to never miss any of my new releases.

Check out a teaser from my next book, To My Brother's Cocky Best Friend Below.

Dear Tyler,

This morning in the shower you heard me singing You're so Vain, by Carly Simon? And it's quite apropos because I bet you think that song was about you! And let me clarify when I sang it this morning, it was about you because we both know you're the most vain, conceited, arrogant, pompous guy out there. And no, I have no interest in coming to Florida to watch you play basketball with your league next week. Haven't you heard white men can't jump?

Olivia

Hey Olivia,

So what you're saying is you're singing songs about me and for me? And you like to watch old movies that stereotype hot men like me?

Tyler

P.S. Come to the game and I'll show you all the things I can't do.

Dear Tyler,

You mean like spell, articulate well, sing, cook, kiss?

Olivia

Olivia,

Give my lips five seconds and I'll show you who can't kiss.

Tyler

Tyler,

Give my feet two seconds and I'll show you who can't kick.

Olivia

Olivia,

So I'm gathering from that statement that you're longing to touch me?

Tyler

P.S. I knew this sexual tension would finally get to you.

Tyler,

You're infuriating. Leave me alone. I have work to do.

Olivia

Olivia,

I have work for you to do as well.

Tyler

P.S. And it includes finishing off what we started last night.

Tyler,

I'm going to show my brother these emails and he's going to be pissed off. I hope your pretty face is ready.

Olivia

Olivia,

I'm always ready for you.

Tyler

P.S. I'm with your brother right now and he's laughing.

Tyler,
And he knows exactly what you're writing and what you said to me last night??
Olivia
P.S. Let him read these emails and see if he's still laughing.

Olivia,
Maybe not. You haven't given me an answer to my question yet.
Your brother's wonderful hot and incredibly intelligent best friend, Tyler.

To My Brother's Cocky Best Friend,
You will never get an answer from me other than no.
Olivia

Olivia,
So I'm taking that as a maybe?
Big Cock Tyler

Tyler,
Goodbye.
Olivia

Olivia,
See you in two hours.
BC Tyler

Olivia,
No response?
BC Tyler

Olivia,
Too busy dreaming about this BC huh?
Tyler

Tyler,
{This photo of a huge penis has been blurred from your screen}
Olivia

Tyler,
> That was a huge cock. You're just a cock-a-doodle-doo.

Olivia

Olivia,
> I've officially been cockshamed. See you at dinner.

Tyler
P.S. I still think you won't be disappointed.

Printed in Great Britain
by Amazon

86937017R00108